Dear Reader:

This is th-
tantes/McCo Hot
SEAL, Black C
Montana Nigh ...book can
stand alone from the others. However, the stories do
tie together and as a reader, I've always enjoyed
catching up with couples from other books in the
series.

The locations for *Christmas in His Arms* are Dallas,
Texas and Bozeman, Montana. Both are, as you realize, real places and cities. But I took creative license to
invent towns, stores, and restaurants that do not exist.

Living in Arkansas, I have been to Dallas
numerous times, as well as have a dear friend who
lives there. Melissa Kinnaird Wise was kind with her
suggestions for locations in *Hot SEAL Black Coffee* and
this book. Any errors about Dallas are either my
mistake or fiction from my imagination.

I have also been to Montana a number of times
and been in and through Bozeman, the town and the
airport. There really is a fireplace at the airport so
check that out! I am also sure the airport crew could
handle any winter weather thrown at them, but it was
better for my couple to have a shutdown of airport
flights, so close it I did. I confess that Bozeman
International Airport is one of my favorite airports.
It's simply cute and welcoming.

Thank you buying the book and I hope you'll
enjoy the entire series.

Cynthia D'Alba

CHRISTMAS IN HIS ARMS

A DALLAS DEBUTANTE/REUNITED
LOVERS/CHRISTMAS STORY

My name is Opal Mae McCool. I love my parents, but
that name? Ugh, but I've adjusted. This year has been
rocking along until October when my entire life lands
in the toilet and someone flushes. First, my groom
dumps me at the altar. Confession...not as destroyed
as I should have been. Then, I share a steamy kiss
with old love which leads to... nothing. Radio silence.
Fine. Disappointed, but moving on. However, it's
almost Christmas and I make a quick overnight business trip to Montana just in time for the snow-
mageddon and I'm stuck in Bozeman with only clean
panties and a toothbrush. Next year has to be better,
right?

I'm Michael Rockland. Born, raised and will die in
Texas and I'm fine with that. I'm a mechanic at heart,
even if my everyday job doesn't allow me under the
hood. About a month ago, I discovered I'm the *Friday
Lunch Special* at a local diner. I'd be pissed if it wasn't
for a good cause and it hadn't led me back to the love
of my life. One hot, steamy kiss, a promise for the

future, and she shuts me out. Harsh, but I'm a big boy. I can deal with reality, except when she ends up on my grandparents' doorstep in Montana.

My dad doesn't approve of him. His mother doesn't approve of me. It's not quite the Capulets and Montagues, and we are long past the teenage years, so isn't it time to let us decide if we belong together or not?

CHRISTMAS IN HIS ARMS

DALLAS DEBUTANTS / MCCOOL FAMILY
TRILOGY

CYNTHIA D'ALBA

Enjoy &
Merry Christmas
Cynthia D'Alba

PRAISE FOR CYNTHIA D'ALBA

An emotional, complex and beautiful story of love and life and how it can all change in a heartbeat.

—DiDi, Guilty Pleasures Book Reviews on *Texas Lullaby*

Highly recommend to all fans of hot cowboys, firefighters, and romance.

—Emily, Goodreads on *Saddles and Soot*

This author does an amazing job of keeping readers on their toes while maintaining a natural flow to the story.

—RT Book Reviews on *Texas Hustle*

Cynthia D'Alba's *Texas Fandango* from Samhain lets readers enjoy the sensual fun in the sun [...] This latest offering gives readers a sexy escape and a reason to seek out D'Alba's earlier titles.

—Library Journal Reviews on *Texas Fandango*

[...] inclusions that stand out for all the right reasons is Cynthia D'Alba's clever *Backstage Pass*

—Publisher's Weekly on *Backstage Pass* in *Cowboy Heat*

Texas Two Step kept me on an emotional roller coaster [...] an emotionally charged romance, with well-developed characters and an engaging secondary cast. A quarter of the way into the book I added Ms. D'Alba to my auto-buys.

—5 Stars and Recommended Read, Guilty Pleasure Book Reviews on *Texas Two Step*

[..]Loved this book...characters came alive. They had depth, interest and completeness. But more than the romance and sex which were great, there are connections with family and friends which makes this story so much more than a story about two people.

—Night Owl Romance 5 STARS! A TOP PICK *on Texas Bossa Nova*

Wow, what an amazing romance novel. *Texas Lullaby* is an impassioned, well-written book with a genuine love story that took hold of my heart and soul from the very beginning.

—LJT, Amazon Reviews, on *Texas Lullaby*

Texas Lullaby is a refreshing departure from the traditional romance plot in that it features an already committed couple.

—Tangled Hearts Book Reviews on *Texas Lullaby*

[...]sexy, contemporary western has it all. Scorching sex, a loving family and suspenseful danger. Oh, yeah!

ALSO BY CYNTHIA D'ALBA

Hot SEAL, Alaskan Nights

Hot SEAL, Confirmed Bachelor

Brotherhood Protectors

(Part of Elle James Brotherhood Series)

Texas Ranger Rescue

Texas Marine Mayhem

COPYRIGHT

Chapter 1

Mae

"You look stunning."

I glanced into the mirror as my cousin Wendy adjusted my bridal veil. With skepticism, I met her gaze in the reflection.

"I'm serious," Wendy said. "You've never looked more radiant than you do at this moment, well, except maybe the night of your debutante presentation. You were radiant that evening."

"And the good thing about my wedding is I don't have to fear the Dallas Debutante Dip." I laughed even as a shiver of fear ran down my spine at the memory of learning, and performing, the graceful curtsey that took every Dallas Debutante downward, close enough that her forehead could touch the floor, or at least should, if done properly. Thank goodness for my big hair that night. I'd faked the floor touch without anyone knowing. Whew.

"I don't know why you two go on and on about that silly bow. It wasn't that difficult," her other cousin Risa said.

Wendy turned to look at her twin sister. "You couldn't do the dip at this moment if your life depended on it."

Risa giggled as she placed both her hands on her protruding, and very pregnant, belly. "I believe you have a valid point. I can barely stand from sitting. Getting up from the floor would be impossible."

"Not without a crane," her sister quipped.

As I watched my twin cousins take playful jabs at each other, I envied their tight relationship. As an only child, I'd been blessed with every possible advantage in life. Money. Great parents. Excellent education. Passable looks.

Every advantage as long as you didn't consider my name. I mean, I was proud to be named after my great-grandmothers, but growing up I would've given anything to be a Tiffany, or Dawn, or plain ole Mary. Still, no one called me Opal, or Opal Mae, or Opal Mae McCool—unless they were family or trying to pull my chain. To all my friends, I was simply Mae.

"You know what?" I said, swiveling on the stool to face my maid and matron of honor. "I envy you two."

"Us?" Wendy said.

"Why?" Risa asked at the same time.

"You've always had each other, watched out for each other. I always wished I'd had a sister like one of you."

"Aw, honey," Wendy said, putting her arm around my shoulders. "You say that now, but Risa was hell to grow up with. All my boyfriends wanted to date her, and when they couldn't, took me instead."

Risa laughed. "That is not true. Don't listen to her, Mae."

I chuckled. "See? I missed having someone to argue with."

Wendy grew serious. "Weren't we mostly around for you growing up? I mean, we tried to be, didn't we, Risa?"

Risa nodded. "Since we were five when you were born, you were like the best doll we ever had."

"Mom said you two carried me everywhere. Tried to dress me up and push me in a carriage." I smiled at the memory. Risa and Wendy had always been a part of my life, like big sisters who didn't live in my house, but were always there when I needed them.

"I remember begging our mom to take us over to Aunt Alice and Uncle Gordon's house to play," Risa said with a sigh.

A knock at the door interrupted their chatter, and the wedding planner's head popped into the opening. "You ready? It's time."

I rose and drew in a deep breath, trying to calm my nerves. I was getting married and was scared to death, but every bride feels the same way on her wedding day, right? "I'm ready." I heard the quiver in my voice.

Wendy was the only one who really understood what my future as a Livingston might entail. She laid a hand on my shoulder. "Nervous?"

I shrugged. "A little. Marrying into the Livingston

family is a big deal." I crossed my fingers and held them up. "Wish me luck."

Wendy hugged me. "Oh, honey. You don't need luck. You have love. The whole Livingston family adores you. Roy is lucky to have found you."

"You think?" I press my hands against my quivering stomach. "I hope so. Without you, I surely wouldn't be standing here today."

"Maybe I pushed a little for a first date, but after that, it was all you." Wendy laid her head against the side of mine.

"Still, I can't believe all the things you did to help him get ready for the wedding. The tux fittings. Getting his hair styled." I held out my arm and a thick, diamond-encrusted bracelet sparkled in the late afternoon light. "Picking out this incredible diamond bracelet as my wedding present."

Wendy feigned surprised. "How do you know I picked out that bracelet? Maybe Roy did it all on his own."

I gave a little snort. "Yeah, I don't think so. He's not that versed in jewelry."

Wendy scrunched her nose. "Well, maybe I helped him a little."

"I heard his bachelor party was a huge hit," Risa said. "Trevor said you did a great job setting that up."

Wendy shrugged. "I felt for Roy. With Everett gone so much, it's not like his best man could help out, and someone had to do it." She grinned. "And I know for a fact there were no strippers."

My dad stepped into the room and tapped the face of his watch. "Let's move it, ladies. Don't want to be late for the wedding."

"Not like they'll start without me," I joked, but that nervous quiver still shook in my throat. I took my dad's arm. "It's now or never. Lead on."

Dad and I stood out of sight from the opened double doors and watched as Risa made her way down the aisle as my matron-of-honor. I had to smile at her pregnant waddle, her floral bouquet not beginning to cover her protruding abdomen.

Wendy glided down the rose-petal-strewn carpet as though she were walking on air. I loved my cousin. For the past year, Roy and I had doubled dated often with Wendy and Everett, Roy's older brother. Everett's job took him out of town almost every week, so Wendy had stepped in to help Everett with his best man duties. I really owed her big time. First, she'd introduced me to my future husband, and then she'd performed all the duties for both the maid-of-honor and the best man. She could've asked me for anything, and I would've gotten it for her.

Dad lightly kissed my cheek. "You nervous?"

I nodded.

"You don't have to do this if you don't want. We can walk out the door, get in the car, and go home."

Turning to him, I laughed. "I want to do this, but thank you for telling me that no matter what, you're there for me."

"In that case, I hope you'll be as happy as your mother and I have been," he said, his eyes growing misty.

"Me, too, Daddy."

As we walked down the church aisle, I saw so many of my friends and extended family. My heart swelled with pride and gratitude that so many people had given up their Saturday to attend my wedding.

My gaze swept the front of the church, expecting to see Roy watching me approach, but he wasn't. He was looking across the room. As I looked at him, his head turned toward me and he smiled, but then he looked across the room again. What had his attention? With everyone standing for my entrance, I couldn't twist my head around and try to find what he was looking at. And even if I could, I'd never be able to see around all the heads in the crowd. There had to be at least five hundred people packed into the Greater Dallas Methodist Church, which wasn't surprising given that a McCool was marrying a Livingston. Either name alone would provide a draw, but both names together were too much for society to ignore.

Roy finally looked at me and smiled. I pasted on a smile as Dad and I stopped near him. My cheeks quivered from the smiling. The pastor started his spiel about marriage, and when he came to the part about who gives this woman to be with this man, my dad spoke.

He was supposed to say, "Her mother and I do," but he didn't. Instead he said, "My daughter is a mature woman. She does not need me nor her mother to give her away. She makes her own decisions, and we stand with her. Therefore, her mother and I welcome the man she has chosen as her husband into our family."

With that, he kissed my cheek and joined my mother in the front pew.

I hope my mouth didn't drop in shock. I have

never been so touched by his public declaration that he and Mom would welcome Roy into our family. They'd never been completely in love with the idea that I was marrying Roy, but this was their way of publicly supporting my decision. My vision blurred with tears. My parents were the best.

I turned toward Wendy to hand off my bridal bouquet. She smiled and winked. I smiled and winked in return. I turned back to Roy, and we joined hands.

His hands were damp and cold. His fingers shook as he held mine. I was pleasantly surprised and secretly pleased that he was as nervous as I was.

I'd been with Roy for over a year, and he wasn't an emotional person. In fact, there had never been passionate expressions of love and need from him. But he'd explained that once he'd hit thirty, he felt he'd matured beyond such childish declarations. At first, I'd been a little disappointed and hurt, until I'd remembered Michael Rockland.

Michael and I had had a passionate and crazy-in-love affair the summer after I'd graduated high school. It'd continued until Christmas of my freshman year of college. It'd been fiery and frantic, as though we'd wanted to be inside each other's skin.

When Michael left me, I'd been emotionally destroyed. I'd decided that what I wanted in a life mate was calmness, patience, and reliability and that stability in that relationship would be more important than emotive outbursts and sex so hot the sheets caught fire.

And that's what I'd spent these last ten years looking for and found in Roy.

As the pastor droned on about love, honor, and family, Roy's face continued to be somber, but his eyes kept shifting around as though he were looking past me. Abruptly, he dropped my hands and stepped back. "I can't do this," he said. "I'm sorry, Mae."

A gasp rumbled through the onlookers.

"I don't understand. What's going on, Roy?" My brain fogged with confusion. I frowned as my stomach clenched and my heart skittered and fluttered with shock.

A sheen of sweat popped onto his brow. "I'm so sorry. Really, I am, but..." He looked past me again, and then his gaze met mine. "I've fallen in love with someone else."

This time, the gasp from the crowd was much louder.

"I'm sorry, you did what?" My emotionally unavailable fiancé had just announced to the world he'd found love with someone else? *What the hell was he talking about?* "Who? When? Where? How?"

I didn't need the audio system set up to convey our vows throughout the chapel to relay my shock. I'm sure my voice carried to the rear pew without the need for amplification.

"I'm sorry. I can't ignore what I feel, what I know she feels, too. We would never hurt you, but when love is this strong, I can't pretend it doesn't exist."

The tang of nausea tickled the back of my throat, and I feared I was going to spew waffles and bacon all over his tux and my beautiful Vera Wang gown. My head swam. My stomach roiled, threatening again to shove my brunch back up my throat.

Then, to my shock, he stepped back and walked

past me. I whirled around to see where he was going, well, whirled as best one could in a floor-length bridal gown with a four-foot train. My eyes opened wide, and my mouth gaped as he walked up to my maid-of-honor.

"I love you," he said to Wendy. "I love you with all my heart and soul. I can't stop thinking about you, dreaming about you." He reached for Wendy's hand. "I know you feel it, too."

"What?" Wendy screeched and jerked her hand back. "What are you talking about?"

"Yeah, Roy," I said. "What the hell are you talking about?"

The pastor gasped at my use of the word *hell*, but he should have been glad I didn't say fuck...or hadn't, up to this point.

Out of the corner of my eye, I saw my dad rise. I was pretty sure he was getting ready to kill Roy, who continued to dig his own grave.

"Us. You and me. Together," Roy said, his expression beseeching. "I love you with all my heart."

He again reached for Wendy's hand.

She again jerked it back, only with more force this time.

Great. My non-emotive fiancé was finally ready to be passionate and publicly declare his love. Unfortunately, it was to my cousin, not me.

Wendy's startled eyes met mine, and she shrugged. She looked back at my errant groom. "Roy. I don't know what's going on in your pea brain, but I think we need to clear something up." She grabbed his arm and pulled him across the church sanctuary then through an exit door.

I looked at Roy's best man, his brother Everett. "What the hell is going on?"

He frowned. "I have no idea, but I'm going to find out."

Everett started toward the door.

"Not without me, you're not," I shouted. Hiking up my dress, I followed him across the room.

"We'll be back," I shouted over my shoulder to the crowd. "Keep everyone else away," I said to Risa as I raced past.

She nodded.

We reached the outside courtyard in time to hear Wendy say, "Roy. You don't love me. I don't love you. I love my cousin Mae. Everything I did to help you was for her, not as some excuse to spend time with you."

"You can't mean that. You made sure I was always on your dates with my brother. You took me to your hair stylist. You kissed me."

My heart shattered inside my chest. "You kissed him?"

"You kissed my brother?" Everett said at the same time.

Wendy blew out a breath. "*On the cheek.* Everyone calm down. I didn't *kiss* kiss him. I brushed his cheek during the tux fitting." She reached for my hands and squeezed my fingers. "I would never *ever* do anything that would hurt you. Ever. With Everett's job taking him away so much, I wanted you and Roy to have the fantasy wedding, including a bachelor party for him. I tried to make everything perfect." She squeezed my hands again, and then glared at Roy. "You are an idiot. To have cold feet is one thing, but to embarrass our families like you did today is unforgivable."

Everett opened his mouth as though he were going to defend his brother, but then shook his head and said nothing.

"What do you want to do, Opal Mae?" Wendy asked. "I'm sure Risa has held off our families as long as she can."

I didn't know. My brain was firing ideas like a machine gun. I sucked in a deep breath and said, "I want Roy to leave. Now."

If nothing else, I was sure I wanted him gone. Even if he suddenly regained his senses and declared he was sorry, even if he said he'd had cold feet but was over that, and he desperately wanted to marry me, I would never even consider it. I needed a steady, faithful, calm man as my soulmate. I thought that was Roy. Obviously, it wasn't.

Roy's shoulders sagged. He looked more like a child who'd been punished for stealing a cookie than a man who'd just destroyed my future.

"Come on, Roy," Everett said with a deep sigh and grabbed his brother by his shoulder. I watched the two men cross the courtyard and exit through the gate.

I closed my eyes, not only to try to collect myself, but to figure out what to do next.

Wendy said, "I can go in and tell everyone the wedding is off if you want me to."

I opened my eyes and shook my head. This was my mess. I needed to fix it. And besides, the last thing I wanted was everyone talking about how destroyed I was today. I needed to be strong, or at least project strength. "No. They were here at my invitation. I'll send them home, and then I need some time."

When I opened the door to the church, I ran into Risa's back. I put my hands on her shoulders. "Thanks, for... you know...holding back the herd."

Risa turned around and hugged me. "I'm so sorry."

"Yeah, me, too."

My heart was racing as I walked back to the front of the church. Thank goodness I had on extra-strength deodorant. I'm sure I was pushing its effectiveness to the max. Maybe I should write the company and tell them this story. I could make an ad for them.

I might have been left at the altar, but my deodorant hadn't left me stranded.

A microphone had been placed at the front of the altar so the audience would hear our vows, although now my words would be completely different.

I cleared my throat and stiffened my back. "Thank you all for coming. I am honored that you would come at my request on a Saturday. As you've probably ascertained, there will be no wedding."

My gaze dropped to Roy's parents who stood with Mom and Dad. "Roy left with Everett. I'm sure they'll be at your house when you get there."

I looked at my parents, and my heart broke seeing the pity in their eyes. I didn't want pity. I didn't need sympathy at being left at the altar nor for my fiancé declaring his love for my cousin. "I'm so sorry, Mom and Dad, but you have to know Wendy did nothing wrong. Roy was the one who got confused."

My mom nodded.

I looked over the five hundred or so guests staring at me. "Thank you for coming. I'm sorry for any inconvenience you went through to come out tonight."

I pushed the microphone back into its holder and walked back to the door that led outside. Risa and Wendy held out their arms to me, and I let them enfold me and lead me outside to cry privately.

As I stood there in the courtyard, I couldn't honestly say if I was crying because I was so upset that I wouldn't spend my life with Roy or crying from the embarrassment of being dumped so publicly. I wish I could said the tears were for Roy, but I can't.

Deep, deep inside me, there was a grain of relief. I couldn't, or wouldn't, admit that maybe, just maybe, fate had saved me from a huge mistake.

Chapter 2

~

Mae

~

My cell phone vibrated a jig across my desk. I picked it up and swiped across the screen. "This is McCool."

"It's time, Mae."

I leaned back in my chair with a smile. "Time for what?"

"Time for you to quit hiding in your office or your apartment, or wherever you've been hiding."

Ouch! Leave it to KatiLyn Cooper to call me out on my excuses. Everyone else treated me with kid gloves, as though I might burst into tears any second.

Which I wouldn't.

KatiLyn and I had been friends and roommates

during college, and then law school. She might have understood me better than I did.

"It's time for you to rejoin the world," she continued.

"And how do you know I haven't rejoined the world, as you said?"

"Because you missed Jack and Suzanne's Halloween party last weekend. Everyone was there except you, and you never miss that party."

"I know," I said with a sigh. "Did I miss anything?"

"I'm not telling you on the phone. You have to go to lunch with me if you want to find out all the gossip."

I chuckled. "Well, with an offer like that, how can I refuse?"

"Great. I'll be there to pick you up at eleven."

"I can meet you. Name a place."

"Nope. I'm taking you somewhere different. There's a ten-dollar lunch special I think you'll find interesting."

"Now, you've got me curious."

She laughed. "See you in an hour. Oh, and we'll be gone longer than usual, so you might want to let your assistant know."

"Okay. See you then."

I hung up the phone with a shake of my head. KatiLyn was always the planner of events sure to get us in trouble. I wondered what she'd cooked up for today. But she was right. I did need to get back to a life that involved more than work and reality television.

A little before eleven, I took the elevator from the fifty-first floor to the lobby. As I walked through the main exit, a red Ferrari convertible whipped into the passenger loading zone and stopped.

KatiLyn waved through the open top. "You like? Dad surprised me with it for my birthday."

"Are you kidding? Who wouldn't?" I said, admiring the flashy car. It wasn't something I would want or drive, but the car was perfect for her.

She grinned. "I know it's a little over the top, but there are advantages to being the baby of the family. Hop in."

I climbed in and looked around. The caramel-colored leather was warm from the Texas sunshine. As I snuggled into the material, the soft seat caressed my tush while heat soaked into my tense gluts. The effect was a relaxing of muscles along my spine. I made a mental note to call for a massage ASAP.

Sighing, I stroked the leather on the dash. "Kati-Lyn, this is fabulous."

"Thanks." She punched the engine and roared back onto the street.

I laughed. "I like your Friday lunch special. Good surprise."

"Oh, this isn't the lunch special. Just hang tight, girl. You'll enjoy that, or at least be intrigued."

KatiLyn headed toward southwest Dallas, an area I hadn't been to in years and definitely not the fashionable lunch area KatiLyn preferred. During the twenty-minute drive, KatiLyn filled me in on all I'd missed over the three weeks since my wedding debacle. And while she had me laughing with her stories, especially about last weekend's Halloween party, deep down I didn't feel as though I'd missed much. In fact, most of her stories made me realize how much in a rut my life had been.

But heavy thinking was for another time. Today in the November sunshine with my BFF, I just wanted to relax and enjoy.

KatiLyn whipped into the parking lot of Maude's Diner and found a spot between a Bentley and a Mercedes.

"We're here," she announced with a bright smile.

"Seriously?" I looked around a parking lot of expensive cars, not one of them under a one-hundred-thousand dollar starting sales price. "What's the deal? What's with all the expensive cars?"

"The ten-dollar lunch special. Come on. I hope we get a table."

I followed her into what could best be described as a "greasy spoon" diner. The scent of expensive perfumes and cooking grease greeted us at the door. The black and white linoleum under my feet was chipped in spots, with the white being mostly an aged-yellow. There were about fifteen tables, each one occupied by young, attractive women dressed in pricey outfits. There wasn't a face without perfect makeup, except for the three ladies dressed in classic pink waitress uniforms working the eatery. A row of ten stools stood in front of a long eating counter, which faced the waitresses' work area and kitchen window. A glass of iced tea or a cup of coffee sat in front of each patron.

"Yay. We got lucky," KatiLyn announced as she race-walked to the last empty table.

The table wasn't in a prime location by any definition. Stuck in the back corner, the two of us could barely squeeze into the chairs.

"I am so confused," I said with a frown.

"Don't worry. All will become clear very soon."

My stomach growled, and I reached for the plastic menu standing upright between the napkin holder and the bottle of ketchup. The menu had nothing on it that would, in my opinion, draw so many women for lunch. Most of the offerings were deep fried. I suspected the cook could deep fry a salad, if requested.

The roar of a motorcycle in the parking lot had all the ladies fluffing their hair and arching their backs to project their assets. An excited chattering rose among the tables.

I glanced over at the waitresses behind the bar and watched as the oldest one shook her head and turned to speak through the kitchen window to the male cook.

The door opened, and *he* swaggered in. Dressed in ass-hugging jeans, a black leather jacket pulled tight around his broad shoulders, and a pair of thick-soled motorcycle boots, his presence seemed to suck the air from the room, or possibly the lack of oxygen might be related to my own inability to draw in a breath. His shiny, dark hair was disheveled as though he'd just run his fingers through it...pretty much what I suspected every woman in this room wanted to do. His cheeks and jaw sported a scruff that brought a tingle to the junction between my thighs at the thought of that soft stubble abrading the tender skin there.

Except, I didn't have to imagine what that would feel like. I knew.

I grabbed KatiLyn's knee and squeezed...pretty hard, if her noisy intake of breath was any indication.

I tossed a frown at KatiLyn and mouthed, *What the fuck?*

Her only reply was to squeeze my hand before prying my dug-in fingers out of her flesh.

"Hey, Maude," he said, his voice deep and rough with testosterone and sex appeal. "Is my lunch ready?"

"Almost. Give me a minute."

"Anything for you," he said to the older woman.

My heart tapped out an SOS on my chest wall. My breathing stuttered, and my stomach rolled over. My fight or flight response kicked in, and I fought the urge to run.

Thank goodness, I was seated in the corner. The odds were he would never see me.

Why was I so bothered by seeing him? Why didn't I jump up and run over to say hi? It'd been ten years, and we'd been friends, right?

Was it because my legs had turned to jelly and wouldn't support my weight?

Or was I embarrassed to be sitting here with all these bored, rich women who had nothing better to do than drink a glass of tea while ogling a man who'd only come in to get his lunch?

He glanced around the café, smiled at the women, acknowledged his audience with a slight nod. But he couldn't just give them a simple smile. Oh no. He had to pour out his panty-melting smile that no woman could resist.

His gaze swept past our table to the next. And then he froze. His head and gaze returned to me. He lifted one eyebrow in my direction then collected his lunch and sauntered back out the door.

The second the door closed, I released a breath I didn't realize I'd been holding. I heard other women doing the same.

He hadn't changed much since high school. Ten years older. A body that was definitely more man than boy. The cocky attitude was still there in spades.

At the sound of his motorcycle roaring from the lot, the women stood, each one tossing a ten-dollar bill onto the table before tottering on high heels out to their cars.

KatiLyn stood, and I jerked her back into her chair. "Why did you bring me here? You know who that is, right?"

She sighed. "Of course, I know who he is."

"Then why?"

"You needed to be reminded that you'd loved someone before Roy-the-Asshole lost his mind at your wedding. You'll fall in love again. Your life didn't end in that church."

My lips pressed into a straight line. She had no idea what she'd done, the gaping hole in my chest she'd kicked open with her Christian Louboutin shoes.

"I remember the days after you two broke up," she continued. "The tears. The sleepless nights. The endless questions. It took time, but you got over him. You'll get past Roy's treachery, too."

Quietly, I snorted and shook my head. She *really* had no clue. Ten years ago, when Michael had walked out of my life without a backward glance, I'd delivered an award-winning performance. My recovery from that breakup had been so convincing, even my best friend, who knew me better than anyone, believed it.

She didn't get it, not then and not now. No one got *over* Michael Rockland. You just learned to live without him in your life.

Now, getting over Roy Livingston? Oh yeah. I think the whole embarrassing debacle helped extinguish any feelings for him I'd had. If only he would have said something to me—to anyone—before we were all standing in front of hundreds of people.

"Ready to go?" she asked as she stood and dropped a ten-dollar bill on the table.

I looked up at her with a frown. "I still don't understand. Aren't we having lunch?"

Her eyes opened wide with shock. "Did you read that menu you were holding? There's not a thing on there that's on my diet...or yours, come to think of it." She took my arm and led me toward the door. "I thought we could head over to The Garden for some salads."

I sighed and let her guide me out. Maybe I should be eating more salads and fewer drive-through fast foods. I'd been a dieting fiend before my wedding. Lately, however, maybe...okay, I *had* slid back into some unhealthy eating habits. And *maybe*, I'd put on a pound or two, but I didn't think it showed.

Still, a salad wouldn't kill me, right?

As soon as we were buckled into her car, KatiLyn said, "He's still got the goods, huh?"

I wasn't going to address his goods, not verbally

and hopefully not in my mind either. "How did you hear about this?"

She laughed and nudged my shoulder before zipping out of the lot. "Becca James. You know she's always on the lookout for some hot, new guy."

"How long has this been going on?"

"I don't know. Two, three weeks maybe? Don't worry about Rock. I'm sure he loves it."

At the mention of his nickname, my heart flopped over. "And how did you and Becca get on the subject of my old boyfriend?"

"This car belonged to some fool who raced it and blew the engine. He sold it to Dad for a song. Dad took it to Rock and had him rebuild the engine. From what Dad said, there's nobody who knows more about the engines of expensive imports in this area."

"And again, Becca and you talking about Michael? How did that come to about?"

She shrugged and turned into The Garden parking lot. "He worked on Sally Denton's car, and I'm sure that's how this little Friday special came to be. Sally told Becca, and it went from there. From what I heard, the owner, that Maude person, insisted after the first week, everyone had to order a minimum of ten dollars or get out." She laughed. "Most expensive glass of iced tea in Dallas, but every one of those bitches can afford it. Now, let's grab some rabbit food. I'm starving."

Law school had developed my skills to the point where hiding emotions and expressions were second nature to me. But holding on after a door to my past I'd believed closed, locked, and nailed shut was blown open? Hand me my Oscar!

Chapter 3

❧

Rock

❧

I absolutely hated Fridays. I'd have stopped going to Maude's Diner if she hadn't been Mel's wife. Plus, I sort of owed her for being a second mom. Growing up, Mel and Maude's house, or more accurately, Mel's garage had been my second home. I was never the smartest kid in school, but the first time Mel let me tinker under the hood of a car, I'd fallen in love. My parents had wanted me to go to college to get a business degree, and then join my dad's insurance company. However, the idea of wearing a suit and sitting behind a desk made my dick shrivel.

On the other hand, being under the hood of any car made my engine rev, if you get what I mean.

Now, back to why I hated Fridays. Those ridiculous women sitting there at Maude's like there's going to be a play performance, not to mention their throat-clogging perfumes. I'd told Maude to make them leave, but she said it was bad business to run off customers. Instead, she charged them ten bucks to watch me pick up my lunch. Of course, the money was for the iced teas or coffees sitting in front of them, not that any of them drank anything that I could tell. And from their skin and bones appearances, not many of them ate very often either.

Again, if I hadn't owed Maude...

However, today's lunch run had zapped me like hot electrical wires. Opal Mae McCool, aka Mae as everyone called her, sat at a corner table. I wasn't sure if I should be flattered that she'd paid ten dollars to see something she'd already seen close up and personal, or if her being there was an accident. If the expression on her face was any indication, she hadn't been expecting to see me either.

I parked Betty, my Ducati, behind the shop and let myself into my office through a rear entrance, leaving the door to the store firmly locked. The staff knew not to bother me during lunch unless it was important, but I'd found over the years that what was important to them wasn't necessarily so to me, thus the locked door. It didn't always keep them out, but it did encourage them to solve their own problems before involving me.

As I gnawed on the turkey club sandwich, I thought about the girl who'd never left my mind, and some might say, my heart. Mae had been, and still was, out of my league. If I hadn't needed an English tutor to graduate high school, I doubted she would have ever looked my way. But I had and she had, and the next thing I knew, I was over my head with feelings I didn't know what to do with.

The summer after high school, in the three months before she left for college and for a few sporadic weekends in the fall, she'd been mine. Any spare time I'd had, I'd wanted to be with her. It could've been a movie, or just holding hands watching television. I hadn't cared. I'd planned everything around being with her.

I had loved her with a fierceness that had frightened me, and honestly, still does if I give much thought to it. I'd always known our time was limited. I'd known that at college she'd meet guys who were better educated than I'd ever be, guys with money and manners, guys who had impressive future careers. Guys she could take home to her billionaire parents.

Not a guy like me.

I'd only met her parents a few times, and I'd understood her reluctance about being with me around them. I was her last high school fling before moving on to bigger and better. She'd never said that, of course. She'd said we'd see each other when she came home, or I could come to Austin to see her.

At the memory, I shook my head and guzzled a drink from my water bottle. Me, on a college campus. I couldn't see it. I was sure she'd said those things to make me feel better, less rejected when she left, and she did leave.

But at her invitation and insistence, I did make the trip to Austin for a couple of weekends. I hadn't had the time, money, or, initially, the transportation, so I'd begged rides and saved money in between visits. I didn't come from a poor family. My dad sold insurance, and my mom taught second grade, so we were a solidly middle-class family. But Mae's family was in an economic class of their own. And while she'd said money didn't matter to her, don't all rich people say that?

We hadn't gone out much when I came up to Austin to see her. Mostly, we stayed in, ordered pizza, and watched movies. And when we had gone to a couple of football games, I'd quickly realized that I didn't fit in, and would never fit in, with her college crowd. Her crowd had been khaki-wearing, starched oxford shirt-wearing types with professionally cut hair and soft, smooth hands.

Then as now, I was a jeans guy, and typically a jeans guy with an oil-stained shirt, hair in need of a trim, and motor grease under my nails.

Instead of going to college, I'd mostly stayed in Diamond Lakes, worked for Mel, and taught myself the ins and outs of every type of engine.

I washed down the last bite of sandwich with a gulp of water, tossed the lunch sack into the trash, and unlocked my door. When I opened it, the sales manager, service manager, and two mechanics were standing in a line.

I sighed. "Okay, who fucked up what?"

A week later, Friday morning had been the kind of morning that usually happened on Monday. Lost paperwork. Scratched doors. Even a lovers' spat between salespeople. That one, I wouldn't touch with a ten-foot pole.

Most people didn't know I was the majority partner in Regency Motors, a dealership that sold and maintained used high-dollar imported brands such as Bentley, Rolls Royce, Maserati, and some lesser expensive makes like Jaguar and Range Rover. I'd been lucky in business and in the right place at the right time.

My partner, Howard Greenblatt, was our public face. He did the ads. He did the handshaking. He did the public service. I preferred to stay in the background, and more importantly, the shop. In fact, there were days I spent working on complicated engines or teaching my mechanics some new technique.

For the most part, I was living my perfect life. However, my personal life was fairly non-existent, a fact that drove my mother crazy.

As I said, Friday morning had been a series of frustrations. The last thing I wanted to do was present myself at Maude's Dinner like a prize stud. In fact, I was tired of being treated like a piece of prime beef.

It was after eleven-thirty when I called Maude.

"Maude's Diner," a perky voice answered.

I knew the voice. Patty. Blonde. Sexy. And happily married to a marine and pregnant with a baby due around Christmas. "Morning, Patty."

"Hey yourself, stud," she said with a laugh.

"When are you going to leave your husband and run away with me?" I joked.

"Well, the baby should be here by Christmas, out of the house for college in about eighteen years, so maybe then."

I laughed. "Is Maude around?"

"Sure thing. Hold on."

I held for a minute or so before a raspy voice said, "This is Maude."

"Hey, Beautiful."

"Hey back. Whatcha wantin' for lunch?"

I sighed. I knew Maude pulled in a stupid amount of cash on Fridays—most of which went straight into the needy pockets of the waitresses and James, the cook—but I just couldn't face another Friday show. I had to tell her.

When I didn't say anything for a minute, she blew out a long breath. "Not comin', huh?"

"Maude, you know I'd do anything for you, but don't you think this has run its course?"

"Maybe. There are fewer women here today."

I chuckled. "So, the flavor of the month changed, and I'm out. Thank goodness."

"Hold on."

I heard her holler, "Sorry, ladies. Rock won't be here today."

Then I heard the scrape of chair legs on linoleum and the rustle of people moving.

"Okay, the place is cleared out. Are you really not coming for lunch? You've got to eat, boy. You can come in the back door, and no one would be the wiser."

I smiled. Second mother, indeed. "Work is crazy, so no. I'll grab an apple or something."

"Okay, then."

"Maude."

"What?"

I hesitated, not wanting to tip my hand, but there was no other way to find out what I wanted to know. "Last Friday, there was a blonde in the corner. She was sitting with a fiery redhead. Do you remember?"

"Yep. The redhead had been here before, but the

blonde hadn't. She looked out of place with the rest of those vultures."

"Now, Maude. You're talking about my client base," I said, my tone wry.

She chuckled. "I know. You sell them those fancy cars, but to answer your question, no, the blonde wasn't here."

I nodded, even though she couldn't see the action. "Okay. Thanks."

"Who is she?"

"No clue. Just saw a new face and wondered. Thanks, Maude. I'll be around next week sometime."

Going to Maude's for lunch was not something I did because it was fast and close. It was a thirty-minute drive there and back, but the Friday lunches gave me a chance to check up on Mel's widow. When Mel had died, I'd promised to look after her, and I had, and would continue to do so until she died. At the rate she was going, I worried she would outlive me. I read somewhere that researchers say that the first person to live to one-hundred-and-fifty had already been born. I'm thinking it might be Maude.

After putting the receiver back, the thought of my social life, or lack thereof, left a sour taste on my tongue. I pulled out my cell phone, scrolled through my contacts, and made a date for Saturday. A safe date. A woman I knew who enjoyed a good meal out and maybe a couple of hours at her place with a full understanding of our long-term prospects, which were none.

The Saturday date began okay, but it didn't take me long to realize the whole evening had been a mistake. Sure, dinner was good and the sex was great, if not exactly earth-shattering, but the night hadn't done anything to curb my growing dissatisfaction with everything in my life.

By Sunday, I'd been as restless as a caged tiger. After getting on my own nerves, I'd finally headed down to my private garage and worked until after midnight on the engine of a 1954 Rolls I'd been rebuilding.

When Monday morning came, even I didn't want to be around me. After the third blow-up at an innocent mistake by the finance manager, Howard, my business partner, suggested—rather strongly, I might add—that I go home, take a boxing class, or go work with the mechanics in the shop. I opted for the shop.

The smells. The noise. The hum of the florescent lights. The puzzle that a car's engine can provide. Some, or all of it, pulled me out of my funk. I spent the rest of the week working with the guys.

On Friday, I made my usual appearance at Maude's. The parking lot wasn't cram-packed like it had been so many weeks before, but there were still enough expensive cars to alert me that while there may be a new flavor of the month, some women apparently still had a thing for the blue-collar mechanic. My mind rolled to the question of whether or not I played a starring role in any of their erotic fantasies, but I quickly snubbed out the thought. I didn't want to know.

I glanced around looking for, well, I wasn't sure what. Mae's car? I didn't even know what car she drove. She could afford any car of her choosing. And the only cars that had caught my attention in the past were ones I'd worked on, like that fire-red Ferrari.

Interestingly, it was in the lot today, only the third time I'd seen it.

I climbed off Betty and headed into the diner. Patty stood at the register giving me a wide grin.

"Hi, Rock," she said loudly.

I winced. "Why are you shouting? That baby suck all your hearing genes right out of you?"

She laughed and leaned toward me. I leaned over the counter toward her.

"What?" I asked.

"Oh, nothing," she said with a grin. "The woman in the far booth gave me an extra five if I could get you to lean over the counter."

I jerked upright. "Maude, fire her," I demanded with no heat in the words.

Maude handed me a sack with my Ruben sandwich and chips. "Can't," she said, pushing flyaway strands of gray hair off her brow and shook her head. "She's pregnant. Feds will get me."

Patty gave a gay laugh, grabbed a coffee pot, and went to refill mugs.

"At least tell me I have some cookies in here," I said, taking the white lunch sack.

"Warm chocolate chip and a couple of snickerdoodles left over from yesterday," Maude said with a crisp nod.

I nodded. "Fine, then. You don't have to fire Patty."

I fought the urge to look around the room at the women. Was Mae here? And if she was, should I go over and speak to her?

When I didn't whip around and leave, Maude crooked a finger, and I leaned over the counter again.

"The blonde's not here, if that's what you're wondering."

I lurched upright. "I wasn't wondering. I mean, what woman?"

Maude laughed. "Get out of here. I need to clear the place for some real customers."

I turned toward the room. "Ladies." I tipped an imaginary hat. "Fine day, isn't it? I hope you all have a lovely afternoon."

Then I turned my best feature toward them and left.

I didn't make the same dating mistake that weekend. I called no one. Instead, I slept with only my right hand, my most reliable lover. I continued work on the antique Rolls. She was a beauty, and I was sure Howard would sell it for way over our cost.

Monday morning, I decided that Mae had had enough time to reach out, if she had even a glimmer of interest in reconnecting. I admit, I was disappointed. I'd hoped...but, oh well. Obviously, she was staying in her own social class for dates. At least, I assumed she was back to dating after her almost-wedding seven weeks ago.

At a little after three, Maude called, which is highly unusual. My internal alarms went off.

"Maude? What's wrong? Are you hurt?" were my first three questions after she said my name.

"What? Don't be ridiculous. Of course, I'm not hurt."

I breathed out a sigh of relief. "Okay. What can I do for you?"

"Think you could run by the diner this afternoon?"

Frowning, I said, "Sure, not a problem. Are you positive everything is okay? Patty didn't go into early labor, did she?"

Maude chuckled. "God, you're a mother hen. No, Patty's fine. Her little one is rockin'-and-rollin' around. I just need to ask for a favor, and I'd rather do it in person."

I nodded, pulled my checkbook out from my desk, and ripped out a check. "Glad to help out. You know that. You only have to ask." I was fairly flush with cash these days. Spotting her a loan I had no intention of collecting would be no big deal. I could afford it.

I pulled into Maude's lot at close to five. I'd meant to get here earlier, but life happens. The lot was empty except for the employees' cars and a very fine, hunter green, antique Jaguar.

I took a minute to look over the car before I went in, even going so far as to run my finger along the convertible top. Whoever owned this took great care of the exterior. No dings. No rust. So highly polished I could see my reflection in the door.

Intimately familiar with this model of Jaguar, I knew it could be a bitch to keep running because of its many electrical problems. But if an owner could get those under control, this baby would hold its value due to its classic lines.

When I entered, I saw Maude sitting in the private booth near the kitchen she and her girls used for their meals and breaks. Rarely was it used for customers.

Maude's broad face beamed with a wide smile as she nodded at whomever sat across from her. Her gaze lifted, and she saw me. She waved, and I waved back then pointed to a table as an indication I would wait for her to finish her chat.

She shook her head and gestured me over. I wound my way through the tables and approached the booth.

Only when I got there did I see who was sitting across from her.

Chapter 4

≈

Mae

≈

"Michael, you remember Mae McCool, don't
you?" Maude said, with a grin.

He stood at the edge of the table, his thick fingers
flexing, relaxing, and flexing again. Because of his
height and my seated position, my eye level was even
with his crotch. His jeans had been washed and worn
so many times that the material hugged him in all the
right places. I didn't want to stare at his—*fine*, I'm
lying. I wanted to study every dip, curve, and bulge in
close and intimate detail.

I dragged my gaze from his thighs—yeah, let's call
it his thighs, but my eyes might have shifted a little
left and right—up past the nip at his waist, to the
expanse of his chest to, finally, his face.

My heart skittered to a shuddering stop before pounding painfully against my breastbone. I locked my lips into a smile, even as I was near fainting from not being able to draw a breath.

As I awaited his reply, my brain flashed through response options. If he pretended he didn't know me, should I play along? If he agreed he knew me, should I hold out my hand for a shake? Stand for a hug? Kiss him on the cheek? The mouth?

Or if he fulfilled my worst nightmare and acknowledged knowing me before turning on his heel and walking away, should I go after him? And if I did, what would I say?

"Mae," he said, his voice richer and deeper than it'd been ten years ago.

A shiver ran down my spine. "Michael."

"Well, I can see you two don't need me," Maude said, sliding from the booth. "Bring you something to drink, Rock?"

"What?" Momentary confusion flashed across his face before he pulled his gaze from mine and to Maude's. "Sure. Coke's fine."

"You got it. Refill, Mae?"

I looked at my almost full glass of iced tea. "I'm good. Thank you."

She left, and Michael slid into Maude's place at the booth, the one across from me and not next to me.

An uneasy pause filled the space as we waited for his drink. Finally, a perky, very-pregnant blonde sat a large, fizzing glass of Coke in front of Michael and touched his shoulder.

She glanced at me before asking, "Need anything

else, Rock?" I got the feeling I'd been warned not to do anything that might hurt him.

Michael shook his head. "Thanks, Patty. I'm good."

I could have been wrong about that feeling, but she did give me the stink-eye before waddling away.

Yes, I realized that thinking of her walk as a waddle was cruel, but she'd set a possessive hand on Michael's shoulder and given me the stink-eye, so I felt justified in my cattiness.

"You're looking good," he said.

"Thank you. You, too."

"I'm glad you came back."

"I wanted to talk, but you don't have a phone number listed."

He nodded. "Cell only."

"Me, too."

"I know."

Did that mean he'd tried to call? I wanted to ask, but part of me feared rejection again.

The booth was thick with tension, or maybe I was projecting my own nervousness. He looked cool and unaffected, as if seeing me again was no more nerve-racking than talking with a potential client. I struggled for a topic of discussion, my emotionless acting skills now a thing of the past. Right now was looking like a great time for that nervous breakdown everyone thought I'd had after my non-wedding.

"You're a mechanic?" I asked.

Inside, I groaned. *Great start, Mae.* I sounded like such a rich-bitch snob.

"Among other things."

I shrugged. "I just wondered." I studied his hands folded on the table. "Your hands are, well, so clean."

Oh, my God. I had completely lost my mind and all societal manners.

"I do understand the principles of soap and water." He leaned back in the booth, getting as far away from me as he could, effectively telling me to go fuck myself. Couldn't blame him for that. The stick that was shoved up my ass was showing.

I felt the heat as it rushed to my face. "I didn't mean it that way," I said, all the words coming out in a long gush. "I'm sorry. I guess I'm a little nervous. I mean, we haven't seen each other in ten years."

An unidentifiable emotion swept across his face. His gaze dropped to the tabletop where his hands rested. His fingers drummed on the table a couple of times before he lifted his Coke and took a long drink. My gaze went to his throat as he swallowed, the action reflected in the slide of his Adam's apple up and down. Reflectively, I swallowed too, but my mouth was so dry, there was nothing to go down my throat.

"Look," he began, leaning on the table, "I owe you an apology."

I wanted to say, "Hell yeah, fucker. You broke my heart and crippled my soul ten years ago," but I didn't want him to know that I still felt that punch of pain with that memory. Instead, I frowned and pretended confusion. "For what?"

"For what I did, for how I broke it off with you." He shook his head. "I didn't handle it well." He chuckled harshly. "That might be the understatement of the year. I was a total ass, and I'm sorry."

My heart shook so violently my chest hurt. He had broken my heart back then. Crushed it until I wasn't sure the pain would ever end. I couldn't honestly say I wasn't still a tad ticked-off that he'd broken up with me at Christmas during my freshman year *for my own good*, as he'd explained it at the time.

I had been dating other guys at college. We'd agreed to see others, and I'd assumed he had been, too. I never knew one way or the other about his dating that fall, but when he'd dumped me, I'd accused him of replacing me with some Diamond Lakes skank, not that I'd had anyone in particular in mind. I'd cried. I'd threatened. I'd accused him of using me. I'd pretty much accused him of everything short of shooting President Lincoln. But he'd stood firm that breaking up with me was in my best interests.

And until he'd walked into the café three weeks ago, I hadn't seen him since.

That's not to say I hadn't thought about him. I had. Many times. Sometimes, I'd get out of bed in the morning and wonder if he was awake, too. I'd imagine him calling and begging me to take him back. I'd created scenarios where I'd be on a date with some famous actor, and we'd run into him and then he'd be sorry he'd let me go.

None of these had happened, of course. Our lives had continued on separate paths, not intersecting, until now.

I drew in a deep breath and reached deep for my emotionless lawyer face. "It was a long time ago, Michael. I've moved on."

He looked down at the table, and then back to me. "Still, I am so sorry for hurting you. I could have done it better or waited it out."

He smiled, and I almost had to press my hands to

my stomach to keep it from flipping over. He had the brightest smile. His dimples didn't hurt either.

"Waited what out?"

"Waited for you to dump me. I was an eighteen-year-old kid who was in love for the first time and scared to death that you'd meet other guys and realize how much better you could do than me. I panicked and broke up with you first."

"Oh, Michael. We were so young and dumb, weren't we?" I reached out and placed my fingers on his hand. "But, apology accepted." I squeezed and pulled my hand back to my lap. "Feel better?"

His smile widened, this time reaching to the sparkle in his eyes. "I feel much better. Obviously, you weren't looking to rehash ten years ago, so why did you want to see me?"

I poked my brain for another topic. I didn't want to confess today's visit was just an excuse to talk to him again. And, more importantly, I wasn't ready for him to leave. Part of me remembered what it looked like and felt like to see his back as he walked away. "I saw you here a couple of weeks ago when I came with a friend for lunch."

I certainly wasn't going to confess about the Friday Lunch Special. It was bad enough I'd come with KatiLyn.

"I saw you. I'll admit I was a little surprised to see you here for the Friday Lunch Special." His eyebrow rose as it had that day, as though asking me a question.

My mouth dropped open, and I leaned forward in surprise. "You know about the Friday Lunch Special?"

He shrugged. I waited for him to smile, to assure

me he was in on the joke. Instead, he turned his hands palms up in a hand shrug that said, *What are you gonna do?*

"Do you remember Maude?" he asked.

The change in subjects jarred my brain. I frowned. "Yeah. She was sitting where you are just a few minutes ago." I tapped the side of my head. "Memory like a trap."

He laughed, which calmed the muscle knots in my back.

I smiled and nodded. "Do I remember her face? No. Remember her name, her husband's name? How significant they'd been in your upbringing? Of course."

What I didn't say was that I remembered everything about those months. If it had been important to him, it had been important to me. Michael Rockland memories had a dedicated lobe in my brain.

He took a gulp from his Coke and replaced it on the table. "After Mel died, Maude said she was too young, and had too much life left, to do nothing all day. She used Mel's insurance to buy this diner. It's been, gosh, about seven years now." He glanced around and back to me. "It's doing okay. It gives her purpose, and she enjoys the customers."

"And you help by letting her exploit you on Fridays...?" My voice was a tad snide, and maybe even a little mean and angry. It was beyond wrong that this woman was taking advantage of Michael. I expected him to... Well, I'm not sure what I expected. What I didn't imagine was him to start laughing.

"Isn't the Friday Lunch Special the most ridiculous thing ever?"

"Doesn't that piss you off? Even a little?" I'm sure my face was twisted into a combination mask of confusion, concern and, yes, lust. Couldn't help it. The man still made all my lady parts sit up and beg.

"I know this will sound nuts, but that whole craziness serves a purpose."

I sat back and crossed my arms. "What good could possibly come out of grown women who should know better ogling your ass?"

He grinned, obviously flattered. "My ass? Is it that good? Tell me more."

I sighed. "Shut up and explain."

"Fine," he started. "Women started coming in on Fridays over a month ago. I have no idea why or how they found out about Maude's."

I interrupted. "I think I can answer that. Sally Denton. Too much money, too much time on her hands, and she lacks any social graces. You worked on her car, and this whole Friday Lunch Special was born."

He nodded. "Ah. Sally. I remember her. I had to fend her off with an oil dipstick once."

I laughed, assuming he was making a joke, but knowing Sally...? Nothing surprised me anymore.

"Anyway," he continued, "these women would occupy all the tables, order nothing, just wait until I got lunch, and then leave. When this whole thing started, I might come for my lunch any time between eleven and twelve. I didn't have a set lunch period like I do now. Having an hour of occupied tables who *maybe* ordered a glass of water was bad business for Maude as well as her crew. She couldn't seat paying lunch customers because the tables were taken. And her wait staff wasn't earning tips, because no one was paying for lunch. So, I set a definite time to come and suggested she make them pay for something, like a door charge." He scratched at his facial scruff. "So stupid. Don't these women have anything better to do than come here to gawk at the blue-collar guy?"

Given that I had been one of those women only a couple of weeks ago, I fixed my stare on my iced tea. However, I knew these women. Oh, not each and every one of them, but their types. Rich. Bored. Ready to have sport at someone else's expense.

Internally, I cringed. People who didn't know me might say the same about me. "And the money? Straight to Maude's pocket?" I said, still trying to justify my own participation.

"No," he snapped. His eyes flashed with anger.

I jerked back at his vehement denial.

"Remember Patty who brought me the Coke? Maybe you didn't notice, but she's pregnant. Her husband is overseas on military duty. Our government doesn't pay those guys shit, so making ends meet for them is tough. She's stashing away money to take six weeks off when the baby comes. Half of the money goes to her.

"The cook in the back...?" He gestured with his glass toward the rear of the diner. "James is a disabled vet. Missing one leg and his right eye. Nobody would hire him or give him a chance until Maude did. Some of the money goes to him so he and his wife can live in an apartment instead of their car."

My shoulders slumped as he continued to speak. My ass slid lower on the bench.

"And the other waitress...? The one who was here

on that Friday that you came for the *special*? Her
name is Billy Sue. Her husband beat her so badly he
knocked out her front teeth and broke her nose and
cheek. Maude found her eating out of the diner's
garbage cans because she had no money for food. She
wouldn't go to a women's shelter for help or report her
husband to the police. She was terrified he would find
her. She was sleeping in an abandoned building
about seven blocks from here. Some of the money
goes to her so she can live in a rooming house."

My eyes shut in horror and repulsion at what
these people had been through and what they faced
on a daily basis. I'd seen the stories on the news. I'd
read about people just like these in the newspaper,
but situations like these were so far removed from my
insulated world.

"I...I...I don't know what to say," was the only reply
I could muster.

"Life is harder for some of us." He placed his
warm hand on top of mine. "You are one of the
lucky ones."

My skin heated beneath his. My heart clogged my
throat, and I could barely take a breath. He had
always had that effect on me. One touch, and I melted
like candle wax under a direct flame.

"Billy Sue..." I whispered. "Did she ever have her
husband arrested?"

He pulled back his hand to his side of the booth. A
chill replaced his warmth, and I slid my hand into
my lap.

"She didn't, no. Too terrified of him, but Maude isn't
scared of much. Cops like to get breakfast here, and she

made sure they knew all about her new waitress. The guys are pretty protective of Maude, which makes them protective of anyone Maude cares about. He's in jail for ten years for domestic abuse. We're still working on a divorce for her. The bastard refuses to sign."

My law practice was corporate, not marital law. Silently, I promised to look into how I could help. "Good," I said.

"So, now you know about the Friday Lunch Special." He laughed. "Last Friday, Patty had me lean over so she could whisper in my ear, only to discover she'd gotten an extra five dollars from one of the women for getting me to do it."

I gave him a little frown. "It sounds like sexual harassment to me."

"Doesn't matter to me one way or the other. You don't need to put your lawyer avenging cape on. I could come in the back door if it really bothered me. It doesn't." He shrugged. "All's good, counselor."

I smiled this time.

"So, what were you doing here? The day I saw you," he clarified. "You forget what the goods look like?"

Like I could forget that tight ass and rippled abdomen. I couldn't help but wonder how the man compared to the boy. After all, the boy had been beyond luscious. I could imagine that the man might be addictive.

I tilted my head and rolled my eyes. "KatiLyn...you remember her? We lived together through college and law school. Anyway, she was the one with me that day."

He nodded. "I saw her. Who could forget that mane of fiery red hair?"

Gosh, I hate to admit his comment elbowed the jealousy dragon who lived in my gut. My dragon raised her head and snorted a puff of green smoke. "KatiLyn decided I needed a lunch out and brought me here."

"Working too hard again, Mae?"

I thought about the non-wedding and my work schedule since. No, I hadn't been working harder than usual, more like less. Truth be told, everyone in the department had treated me as though I were a fragile flower who might wilt and die at any moment.

And I was going to stop that beginning tomorrow.

"Not too hard," I replied with a smile. "Besides, I do enjoy being in the family business."

He leaned back and stretched his arms along the top of the booth's stuffed back. "I always knew you were destined for great things."

I smiled. "You always were one of my biggest supporters."

"That I was. Without your help, I might not have graduated from high school."

"Of course, you would have," I said. "You are so much smarter than you give yourself credit for."

My phone chirped, and I held up a finger. "Hold on. Let me see who this is."

A text from my dad flashed on my screen.

Dad: Looking for you. Want to go over a few things before your mom and I leave town. Come home for dinner. We can talk over your mother's meatloaf.

Me: Wish I could but can't tonight. Catch me tomorrow at the office.

Dad: Meet me in my office in the morning. Seven.

Me: GROAN. Have coffee...AND DOUGHNUTS!

Dad: LOL See you at seven.

Michael watched me as I typed replies. I started to let him think I was texting with another guy, but as soon as the thought came into my head, I shook it off. This wasn't high school, and I'd stopped playing games years ago.

"My dad," I explained. "Setting up a meeting with me in the morning."

His eyebrow arched. "You have to set up meetings to see your dad?"

I laughed. "Most of the time, no. He usually has to set up a meeting to see me."

"Busy lady."

I shrugged. "The realities, I guess."

When I'd answered the text, I'd realized we'd been occupying a table at Maude's for over an hour without ordering anything. I looked around the edge of the booth. The place was empty, as in no customers, no Patty, no Maude, no cook. No one.

"Um, did they close the place and leave us here?"

He chuckled. "Yep. Maude doesn't serve dinner. Usually everyone is gone by three, or four at the latest."

"But it was after five when you got here, and they were all still here."

He leaned over the table and winked. "They're a nosey bunch who wanted to see us together."

"And what did they think would happen?"

Chapter 5

❦

Rock

❦

W hat did they think would happen? Mae's question left me scrambling for an answer. I'd been surprised when Maude had introduced me to someone I'd never forgotten and never would. I'm sure my face had reflected the shock that'd reverberated through me. Opal Mae McCool had been my fantasy girl since I'd first laid eyes on her in tenth grade. It'd been our senior year before fate had finally intervened and made her aware of me. Fate being me flunking English, and Mae stepping up to tutor me. But who wants to read Shakespeare when there's a new thriller release just begging to be cracked open?

Now, I sat alone with her in a deserted diner, doors locked, and most of the lights off. What had

Maude been thinking setting up this situation? Did she have any idea how I had longed for this woman? Didn't she remember how tortured I'd been after Mae and I had split? Did she even realize that I was the one who'd left Mae? It had been for Mae's own good. I'd visited her at college for a couple of weekends. Those visits had made me realize that she could do so much better than me. Her future was unlimited, something I couldn't have honestly said about my own.

My question for Maude when I next saw her would be: What were you trying to accomplish? Did you think putting Mae in front of me would make me declare my undying love? Ask her to forget ten years apart and to run away with me?

Mae snapped her fingers in front of my eyes. "Hey. Where'd you go?"

I crossed my arms over my chest, as I had done during most of our time together. It was the only way I could keep from reaching across the table and taking her hand. I'd already done that once, and my palm still burned from the touch. "Trying to think of the right answer to your question," I replied honestly.

She must have thought I was kidding because she laughed and leaned toward me. The sound of her laugh flow through me, and I had to smile. "I think the answer is that they were amusing themselves. What I mean is, I don't bring my dates to Maude's diner...not that this is a date," I blurted.

"So, there are lots of dates?"

I tried to read the expression on her face. Was she teasing? Jealous? Not extremely interested? I hadn't a clue.

"A few," I admitted.

She interlaced her fingers, propped her elbows on the table, and placed her hands under her chin. "Tell me more. Let me live vicariously through you."

I laughed. "I'm sure your life is much more thrilling than my dates. You hungry?"

I didn't know where that question came from. What I knew was I didn't want to talk about other women, and I didn't want this night to end. Not yet.

Her eyes opened wide. "As a matter fact, I could eat. Want to go somewhere?"

I snorted and hitched my thumb toward the kitchen. "Why? We've got a fully supplied diner."

"You cook?"

"I eat. I'm single. I have to know how to cook."

"And Maude?"

"Won't care. Come on. Let's raid the fridge and see what we can find."

My cooking skills were quite limited, to say the least. Grill a steak? Sure. What man couldn't? Mentally, I crossed my fingers that Maude had a couple of thick, prime steaks marinating in the fridge. The fact that she didn't serve steaks made that hope more of a pie-in-the-sky dream than a reality.

I pulled open the fridge door. "Let's see. No steaks marinating. Damn."

Behind me, a soft chuckle sent blood rushing to my groin. Now, I would have stand here until a growing erection eased up. "I see the usual stuff. Eggs. Cheese. Meats. Butter. She brings in fresh veggies every day, so not many here."

"Omelets?" Mae asked.

"You read my mind."

"You know how to make them?"

I glanced over my shoulder, and my heart skipped a beat...or ten. God, she was beautiful. Her eyes sparkled with her smile. She tilted her head and lifted an eyebrow.

"I make a mean omelet," I said, hoping it was true. How hard could it be to fry eggs?

"Great," she replied. "What are we putting in them?"

We—well, actually she—made a couple of delicious loaded omelets with sides of toast and hashbrowns. I discovered she was an excellent cook, while I was a messy, but helpful, assistant.

Over dinner, we talked about high school, her college, and my work, although I didn't mention the part ownership in Regency Motors. I don't know why I omitted that. I mean, it might have impressed her that the underachieving boy she'd once known had grown into a successful man. I still wasn't in her economic class, and never would be, but I could, when the circumstances demanded, afford the best champagne now instead of the five-dollar kind, not that I ever bought champagne. That stuff was nasty. Give me a good beer any day.

I was glad I'd tackled the apology I owed her earlier. It had bothered me for years to remember how poorly I'd handled our breakup. That long-ago weekend had been a good one. Great seats for the University of Texas football game, which they won over their Oklahoma rivals. We'd gone with a group of her friends for pizza and beer afterwards and then back to her apartment. I had enjoyed myself immensely, but over dinner she'd laughed at jokes I didn't get. She and one of the guys had commiserated over an upcoming exam, while she and another guy had talked about the previous weekend's fraternity party. She wasn't being mean or excluding me in any way. She'd simply been discussing her daily life, and I'd realized I had no place in it.

We'd made love, and my heart had wanted to explode with pent-up emotion. That night had been different than all the other times we'd been together. Maybe the intense passion was because I'd known it would be the last time we'd be together. Maybe it was because I'd poured out all my love, hoping to rid my body of that sentiment.

Of course, that hadn't worked. I'd only loved her more.

We'd been lying in her bed, her back pulled tightly against my front. I kissed her neck, drawing her scent deep into my lungs for the last time.

"I love you," she said.

My heart shattered into a million pieces. The time had come, and I had to face reality, even if she couldn't. "Mae. I adore you. You know I do, but..."

Her body stiffened. "But?"

I took a deep breath and jumped in. "We're on two different paths in life. We live in two different worlds. You need to enjoy college. Date. See lots of people. Enjoy this time. Your future has no limits. You don't need me holding you back."

"What?"

Her whispered reply blew the pieces of my shattered heart into my lungs. I could barely draw a breath. "I..." I hesitated, not wanting to hear the words myself. "I won't be coming back. I think we should break up."

She gave a small gasp and pulled from my arms. She stood and whirled to face me, her beautiful naked body glistening in the moonlight streaming through the crack in the blinds. "Are you kidding me? You fuck me, and then you fuck me again with this?"

I slid to the edge of the bed. "Honey, I—"

"Don't," she snapped, holding up one hand. "Don't say another word."

"Let me explain."

Her laugh was harsh. "Don't bother. You got what you came for. Hell, now that I think about it, you got everything you needed from me, right? Passed English. Graduated high school. Had a fucking great summer." She sneered down at me. "Ha ha. Get it? *Fucking* summer?" She put air quotes around fucking.

She grabbed a T-shirt and dropped it over her head. The hem hit right at the luscious curve where her butt met her thigh. I knew how her skin tasted right there. How soft the flesh was. How sweet her juices were on my tongue. Running my lips along that seam filled my erotic dreams.

"Mae—"

"Don't even say my name." She pointed toward the door. "Just get out."

I started to protest the late hour, but hell, I didn't blame her. I hated me, too.

By that time, I had a cheap motorcycle that I'd ridden down. I could leave without the restrictions of someone else's timetable, thank God.

And until I walked into Maude's Diner three weeks ago, I hadn't seen her since that night.

Well, that wasn't exactly true. I had seen her. She

hadn't seen me. Her gaze had been on her groom waiting at the end of the long church aisle.

Roy Livingston was lucky he'd left the church that day before I could find him and beat him into the pile of shit that he was.

When she touched my hand, I was pulled back into the present.

"I need to go," she said. "It's late, and I have a rough week ahead."

I held still. Hating that our evening was ending. "Yeah. Me, too."

We slid from the booth.

"Thank you for dinner," she said.

"My pleasure." That everything omelet might have been the best meal I'd eaten in years. I took her hand. "It was good to see you again."

She ducked her head as she slid a lock of hair behind her ear. "You too, Michael. Maybe we don't have to wait ten years before we talk again."

My heart elbowed my lungs in excitement. She didn't hate me, and she was suggesting we see each other again. I still wasn't good enough for her, but maybe she wouldn't notice. "Let me walk you to your car."

She slung her purse over her shoulder. "You don't have to. I'm parked just outside."

"Where?"

She tilted her head toward the kitchen. "Maude told me it was okay to park in the back."

I smiled. Maude had her park in the darkest part of the lot, or it would be at this time of the night. The diner was in a safe location, and there wasn't a risk to

Mae if she walked to her car alone, but I felt Maude's matchmaking fingers all over this.

"I'll walk you out," I said, my tone gruff. "Let's go through the kitchen. I can make sure everything is off and lock the door behind us."

After I locked up the diner, we walked over to a vintage, hunter-green Jaguar, the one I'd admired earlier.

"Beautiful," I said. Unable to stop myself, I ran my fingers along the classic curves of the 1961 car. When I'd seen the car earlier today, I'd I thought it looked familiar. Now I realized she'd been in my shop a few years back. I'd rebuilt the engine and made a number of minor tweaks and adjustments until she'd purred like a tiger. I'd been a little heartbroken when we'd sold her. I'd given half-a-mind to keeping her. "She's incredible. How long have you had her?"

She unlocked the driver's door and tossed her bag across to the passenger seat. "Present from the folks when I finished law school," she said with a stroke along the convertible roof. "I saw this car when I turned sixteen and begged for one. Dad had laughed and said, 'Sure, kiddo, as soon as you graduate college.' Then he altered the promise to when I got out of law school. It became a long running joke in the family. To say I was surprised to find it in my parking slot at work one day would be an under-statement."

I closed her driver's door and continued holding her hand as I walked around the vehicle.

"How's she running? Giving you any problems?"

"Are you kidding? Marilyn is perfect. Never hiccups. Never stalls. Drives like a dream."

I stopped at the hood and frowned. "Marilyn?"

She laughed. "Sorry. That's what I named her. Marilyn Monroe. A bombshell beauty from the nineteen-sixties. It seemed like an appropriate name."

Nodding, I said, "Sure. Makes sense. Where do you take her when she needs work?"

"Oh, Dad handles that. I really don't know. Someone picks it up and drops it off later." Our gazes met. "I really have to go."

I nodded and walked her back to the driver's door. I hated for the evening to end. Plus, I really wanted to kiss her.

No. I was going to kiss her.

I pulled her to me and wrapped our joined hands around to her back. Her eyes widened, then she stepped into me, pressing herself against my chest. Before I could lean in, she did. She pressed her lips to mine. I traced my tongue along her bottom lip, and she opened her mouth. Our tongues met and tangled. She moaned and leaned on her door. Our mouths continued their feast until she finally broke the connection.

"As much as I hate this, I really do need to leave." She kissed me again. "Thank you for dinner."

"Thank you," I said. "Next time, candlelight and steaks."

She smiled. "Right. Next time."

I opened her door and, reluctantly, let her slip into her car.

The car's engine fired and idled smoothly.

"Good night, Michael."

"Good night, Mae."

As she pulled away, I stood there watching the

car's taillights until she turned right, and she drove out of sight.

I'm not sure how long I just stood there. I'd felt my world shift with tonight's dinner. I just wasn't sure if that shift would be a positive change in my life, or would leave me crushed under her spike heels. The only thing I was sure of was my life train had switched tracks and what laid ahead was unknown.

Chapter 6

≈

Mae

≈

Bozeman, Montana

"Attention please. May I have your attention please? Due to current weather conditions, all flights in and out of Bozeman Yellowstone International airport have been discontinued for the evening."

The message repeated three more times—three more than I needed to hear. I got it the first time. I was stuck in Bozeman, Montana the day before Christmas Eve.

Super.

Just what I needed to make sure my year

continued on its quest to be the shittiest year of
my life.

However, on the bright side, the snow was
beautiful.

On the dark side, the snow was slippery and thick,
and I didn't know how to drive in snow.

On the bright side, I didn't have to drive in it.

On the dark side, I didn't have to drive in it
because I had nowhere to go.

I'd checked out of my hotel after a very successful
meeting, ready to head back to Texas for the
Christmas holidays, not that I had any holiday plans.
My parents had left at Thanksgiving for a six-week
cruise, a reward from my dad to my mom for working
so hard to make my wedding perfect, and as all of
Texas knew, that day had been a train wreck.
However, just because my groom had turned out to be
a jerk didn't mean I wanted to rob Mom of her dream
trip. So, I'd taken over the leadership reins of McCool
Industries and waved *bon voyage* to my parents.

Now, I was stranded in Montana of all places.
Montana! Amazingly, with all my contacts, this was
the one state where I knew no one.

On the bright side, there were only nine days left
in the month with most of them holiday time, and
everyone knew nothing got done between Christmas
and New Year, right? So, my being stuck in bumfuck
back country wouldn't hurt the business too much.

On the dark side, well, I couldn't think of a dark
side to that since I'd pretty much decided that when I
got home to Texas, I'd slide through the rest of the
days in December, just like most of the staff. No
reason to be a salmon trying to swim upstream.

Around me, people were on phones and clicking computer keyboards, probably looking for hotel rooms, or rebooking flights for whenever the airport reopened. I supposed I should be doing the same, but this was the final straw in a long list of final straws since October.

If only I was a crier, I'd find a nice, private place and have a good long cry. However, as I'd discovered with my non-wedding, crying solved nothing, made my face red and blotchy, and was as productive as setting a snowball in an oven on broil.

I dialed my hotel, hoping my room hadn't been rented out yet.

No luck. It was gone.

Super.

I glanced around the gate area—yes, I'd made it through TSA and to the departure gate before getting the good news the flight was cancelled—for an electrical plug, so I could computer surf and find something in the Bozeman area with a room for the night. This was Montana. They were used to dealing with this kind of weather.

Not knowing much about airport closures, I assumed tonight's problem was the snow and ice and a forecast for much more of the same. However, tomorrow in the bright light of day, the airport crew would know exactly how to clear those runways and get me airborne.

After thirty minutes of phone calls and attempts at online booking, I had yet to find a hotel within ten miles of the airport. How could the other passengers have such fast fingers? And why did I let my assistant have this time off? Of course, it would

be after hours back in Texas even if she were
at work.

Why wasn't Bozeman International Airport
located in Bozeman instead of up the road in
Belgrade? I had so many questions.

I sighed. Even if I were able to book a hotel farther
away, getting there tonight and back to the airport first
thing in the morning might be a problem, and that
was assuming I could find this elusive available
hotel room.

A violent shiver ran down my spine and, frankly, I
wasn't surprised. Dressed for a professional meeting
held in a heated conference room, I wore a charcoal
pencil skirt, pointy-toe-needled-heel shoes, a silk
blouse and dark-gray jacket. I wasn't exactly prepared
for a snowpocalypse.

On the bright side of being cancelled, I didn't have
luggage to claim since I'd brought only an overnight
carry-on. At least I had clean panties for tomorrow
and a toothbrush.

However, on the dark side, I hadn't packed the first
item of heavy clothing as I'd assumed—incorrectly, it
seemed—that I'd be in and out in under
twenty-four hours.

I was smart enough to realize sitting at a gate with
no departing plane was doing nothing to resolve my
issues, so I picked up my briefcase, grabbed the
handle of my rolling bag, and headed for the lobby.
Surely in this airport there'd be somewhere I could
get a coat, or sweatshirt or—please God—socks
and boots.

Yeah, no.

The stores' shelves were mostly bare after the vultures, I mean, smarter travelers got to them first.

I rubbed my hands together and remembered the fireplace in the lobby. Like everything else, I was late to that party, too. All the chairs circled in front of the massive fireplace were taken. This group of travelers was made of stouter material than I. Thick coats and heavy shoes filled my vision. Children played on the carpeted floor, excited by the adventure of sleeping in an airport.

I wished I shared their joy at the idea of spending my night here. I did not.

I squeezed past the families until I reached the fire and held out my hands in an attempt to melt the ice running in my veins.

"Mae? Mae McCool?"

The deep timbre of the voice sent another wave of shivers down my spine and not because I was cold. I knew that rumbling, sexy voice. I'd heard it in my dreams for years and, in person, only four weeks ago. A man I'd expected to hear from after a scorching kiss and a mention of a future dinner. Instead, it'd been nothing but radio, i.e. cellular, silence.

I turned slowly toward the lobby and braced myself to see him again.

I wasn't prepared for the jolt of lust and longing that wrapped fingers around my stomach and squeezed. My lungs weren't working much better. Each breath sounded—to me—as if my throat were the size of a straw. I hoped like heck that my eyes weren't as big as saucers as I studied him.

Dressed in ass-hugging jeans, black T-shirt, a black

leather jacket pulled snug around his broad shoulders, and a pair of thick-soled hiking boots, his presence seemed to suck the air from the room, or possibly the lack of oxygen might be related to my own inability to draw in a breath. His shiny, dark hair was disheveled as though he'd just run his fingers through it, and if the glances from the females in the area were any indication, many of them would have been happy to stroke each hair back into place. His cheeks and jaw sported a scruff that brought on a tingle that leapt from cell to cell inside me.

"Michael?" I hope my voice sounded steadier than my heart felt.

"Mae. What a wonderful surprise," he said, smiling. "What are you doing in Bozeman, Montana?"

"Excuse me," I said to each person I stepped on or climbed over to get to where Michael Rockland stood. As I neared him, I felt a magnetic pull, like the moon had over the tides.

"Hey," I said brightly. "Fancy meeting you here." I shivered again. "Are you here for the fancy dinner you promised?" I tried to keep it light, as though not hearing from him was no big deal, but my teeth clicked together as my mouth chattered in the cold.

"Here." He removed his leather coat and swung it around my shoulders. His hands grasped each side of the neck opening and pulled the heated jacket snuggly around me. "You look like you need this more than I do."

The aroma of clean male drifted into my nose as I burrowed in the warmth. His testosterone seemed to infuse itself into every nook and cranny in my body, or maybe, after ten years, I'd still hadn't been able to rid myself of his essence. Just being this close to him jarred me.

"Thanks," I said, my teeth chattering a little. I pushed my arms down the sleeves and moaned with relief.

"What are you doing in Montana?"

I shook my head with a frown. "It was supposed to be a simple overnight run. McCool Industries is bidding on the airport enlargement, and I needed to be here to research some elements of our bid." I glanced out the window and back at him. "I know. I'm not exactly dressed for the weather."

He chuckled, and the area behind my navel tugged.

"You aren't kidding."

I studied him. "Wait a minute. What are you doing up here? Shouldn't you be in Texas or was there an engine emergency in Bozeman that only you could repair?"

He grinned, and I melted.

"I am pretty damn good," he said.

My stupid libido took that comment and immediately put a picture of him naked in my mind. The next shiver had nothing to do with the cold.

"But," he continued, "I'm pretty sure there are plenty of good engine guys around here."

I pulled his coat tighter, hoping he'd think my erect nipples were from the chill and not from my thrill at seeing him. "So? Bozeman?" I repeated.

"Right," he said with a nod. He hitchhiked a thumb toward the door. "My dad grew up near here. Both his parents passed a couple of years ago, and he inherited their place. He still hasn't decided what to do with it, but the family has been using it like a vacation spot. We were meeting here for Christmas. I came up a little early to open up the house, get the heat going, and so forth. I was supposed to pick them up here tonight."

"Airport's closed for business," I said.

"So I gathered," he murmured.

I squinted up at him. "How'd you get here anyway?"

"Grandpop's old four-wheel drive truck. Beat to hell and back on the exterior, but it runs great. Speaking of his truck, can I give you a lift to your hotel?"

I wrinkled my nose. "I wish. I can't find a room within ten miles of here." I tried to give him a shrug I hoped conveyed a carefreeness I didn't feel. "I'll hang out here. I'm sure the airport will be open in the morning, and I'll get home."

"Mae." He swept his hand from my shoulder to my hip...without touching me, much to my disappointment. "You are not dressed to sleep in an airport. Hell, you're not dressed to be in Montana in December."

I threw up my hands. "I know, Michael." Exasperation rang in my tone. "I don't have any other choices. It's one night. I can put up with anything for one night."

"Except..." He leaned closer. "You don't know it'll be only one night. Could be two or three. This weather isn't normal, even for Montana. Here's my suggestion. Come back to my house, or rather my grandparents' house. There's plenty of room. I'll bring you back when you can fly out."

The idea of sleeping in the same space as Michael Rockland had my heart flittering like hummingbird wings. I wanted to, but I didn't want to. And yes, I heard the voices battling in my head.

"I don't know," I said. "I'd hate to be a burden." While the words passed my lips, every cell in my body was screaming, "She's lying. She does want to come."

And of course, my libido added a snide remark about my needing to come more often.

He scoffed and grabbed my carryon. "Don't be ridiculous. Of course, you'll be a burden. I'll pull through somehow." He turned and started toward the exit. When I didn't immediately follow, he said over his shoulder, "Come on, Mae. You know you don't want to sleep in a cold airport." He pumped his eyebrows with a fake leer. "I promise to keep my hands to myself. Mostly."

I shook my head at his joke. He was right though. I didn't want to spend the night in a drafty airport. So, while I didn't rush to follow him—no reason to let him know I was thrilled he'd taken the decision out of my hands—I did trail him to the door. The closer we got to the exit, the more the ambient temperature dropped.

"How far away are you parked?" I asked, getting worried now.

"Not far, but too far for those heels in this weather. Stay here, and I'll pick you up."

Regretfully, I removed his jacket and held it out. "You'll need this out there."

"You keep it. I'll be fine."

I laughed and shoved the leather into his chest. "Don't be the tough guy. Put this back on."

He gave me the grin I'm sure worked on every female from birth to death. "If you insist." As he pushed his arms into the sleeves and adjusted the material over his broad shoulders, I tried to pull my gaze away, unsuccessfully I might add. Whew. After all these years, his charisma could suck me in like water to a sponge. Struggling against the pull... Well, I might as well have been fighting gravity.

The only question I had was...should I give in to my desires or not?

Chapter 7

~

Rock

~

The air in my lungs froze with my first inhale as I jogged toward my truck. Damn. I needed to get home to Texas. I had no trouble with the blazing Texas heat. But freezing cold weather and I were not friends.

On the other hand, fate had dropped a nice surprise into my life that I would have missed if I hadn't come up to Grandpop's place early.

I'd timed my airport arrival for my parents so I wouldn't be there long, allowing me to park in short term parking. More expensive but definitely closer to the terminal, and tonight, I needed that shorter distance. I'd been happy to give Mae my jacket to warm her up, but I hadn't fought very hard when she'd made me put it back on for the sprint to my truck. My long-sleeve T-shirt wouldn't have been nearly enough.

Snow covered the windshield and hood. I started the truck, set the defroster on high, and climbed back out. Being born and raised in Montana, Grandpop had kept his truck ready for anything, including keeping a long-handled snow scraper under the driver's seat. After tossing Mae's light-weight carryon into the tiny rear seat, I pulled out the scraper and went to work, raking it along the windshield glass. Most of what was there was snow, not ice, so it cleared with minimal effort. I slid behind the steering wheel and realized I'd forgotten to clean off the rear window and the passenger side window. The snow was blowing toward the truck, covering the passenger side more than the driver's side.

Another thing about my Grandpop was he could squeeze a nickel until it screamed, meaning this truck was basic, as in no power windows. Laying across the bench seat, I slowly cranked the handle to lower the glass, trying to make the snow slide off. I got it about one-third of the way down and was startled when a pair of eyes appeared in the opening.

"Open up. I'm freezing."

"Dammit, Mae." Stretching the extra inches to reach the lock button, I caught the black knob between my fingers and jerked it up. I sat up to give her space.

Mae opened the door and climbed into the truck. "Don't start," she said, holding her hand up. "Rookie weather mistake. I know. I thought I'd help you by coming out here, so you didn't have to drive back to the terminal." She shook violently in the seat and held up her fingers to the vents. "Where's the heat?"

"I'm shooting most of it through the defroster." I tilted my head toward the front. Reaching over, I took her hands and wrapped my fingers around her ten little icicles. "I've picked up ice cubes that were warmer," I muttered.

"I know," she said through chattering teeth. "Not my best decision."

My pulse pounded in my ears. As I drew in a deep breath, the scent of cinnamon filled the cab of the truck. Flakes of snow dotted the top of her head, while drops of melted snow dripped down her neck.

"Wait." I pulled my hands away, and I thought I heard her whimper. The sound shot all my blood to my groin. Memories filled my mind even as I tried to bat them away like mosquitoes.

I reached over the seat and fumbled around until I pulled up Grandpop's orange hunting cap. I plopped the florescent hat on her head and pulled down the sheepskin-lined flaps over her ears.

"There," I announced. "That'll help."

What the cap was helping was uncertain. I had hoped she would look ridiculous in it, and that vision would cool my rapidly heating blood. No such luck. The image of her blonde hair flowing out of Grandpop's hunting cap didn't look nearly as ridiculous as I'd hoped. Instead, she looked damned cute.

"Thank you," she said, snugging the earflaps closer.

She'd removed her heels and had her legs stretched out to catch whatever warmth she could from the semi-heated air blowing from the car's heater.

"Hold on." I leaned over the seat again and sent a silent *Thank You* to Grandpop in heaven for the winter emergency pack he'd always kept in his truck. I pulled out a pair of white thermal socks and a small blanket. The two items would serve duel purposes. Help warm her by covering up those sexy legs while, hopefully, cooling me down.

"Put these on," I said, handing her the socks.

She did. They came up to her knees. She sighed. "These feel wonderful."

I'd heard that sigh before, accompanied by similar words, but she hadn't been talking about socks.

I laughed and tucked the blanket around her. "This will help, too."

She snuggled into the wool blanket. "Scratchy, but warm." Looking at me, she said, "Thank you."

"I'm glad I was here to help."

And I meant that. Finally, I could do something for this woman who'd made such a meteor-like impact on my life.

The drive back to Grandpop's place was slow, slick, and hazardous. Sure, the weather was a factor in the slow and slick elements, but the hazardous part was all about my heart. As Mae warmed, the scent of vanilla and cinnamon infused the air in the small space. I forced my concentration to be focused on the road and the driving conditions, but my heart and head wanted desperately to drift in her direction. The tug in my belly was strong and painful, which were descriptions I could have used for my emotions at that moment.

Mae kept quiet on the drive after explaining she wanted my concentration on driving and not talking. Probably—no, definitely a good idea.

Usually the drive from the ranch took maybe thirty minutes on a clear day, but that didn't begin to describe tonight. The sky was dark with clouds. No stars. No moon. In the truck's lights, the road was visible, but only barely through the heavy onslaught of whiteness. There were a few slides and skids, but an hour after we pulled out of the airport parking lot, I turned into Grandpop's drive.

I parked near the rear door in the carport and sat there a moment letting the warm air on the heater blow on my feet. Beside me, Mae exhaled a long stream of air.

"Thanks to you, I have a new talent," she said.

"Yeah?" I looked over at her, and my heart swelled. "What's that?"

"Apparently I can hold my breath for an hour."

I chuckled. "And your tongue."

She blew me a raspberry, which made me laugh again.

"Ready for the dash to the house?" I asked, hiking an eyebrow.

Like many ranches, garages were for expensive tools, like tractors and harvesters, not cars. Those were relegated to carports, sometimes attached, sometimes not. This wasn't, which meant a freezing walk to the house.

"No time like the present." She took off the socks and shoved her feet back into those torture devices women wore.

I confess to checking out her legs while we were at

the airport and, *whew*, they were even better than I remembered.

"I'm keeping the hat and blanket," she said, giving me a hard stare.

I nodded. "Of course, you are. I'll get your overnight bag." I gave her what I hoped was an encouraging thumbs up and opened my door.

Snow covered my hair in only seconds. Tears from the arctic wind filled my eyes and froze on my cheeks. The white flakes on the shoulders of my jacket made it appear I had the worst case of dandruff ever.

I met Mae at the hood of the car without her overnight bag, and I confess, without her permission, lifted her into my arms and race-walked to the house.

"Hey," she protested, even as she draped her arms around my neck. "I can walk."

"I know, but with those shoes, well, the drive to the hospital for a broken leg is something I don't want to do tonight. So, hang tight. We'll be in the house much faster this way."

"But my overnight bag..." she protested.

"I'll come back and get it. Grab the door handle," I said as I climbed the steps.

The door swung open without a squeak or sound, and I walked into the kitchen. When I lowered her legs to the floor, she slid down my body, drawing the attention of my very cold, but now very awake, cock.

"Thanks for the ride," she said, looking up into my face.

Melted snow dripped off her eyelashes and down her cheeks. I wiped away one drip with my thumb. "Wet and exhausted, and you're still the most beautiful woman I've ever known."

Whirling around, I headed back outside to get her bag before I blurted out something even more incriminating. When I got back, she was standing exactly where I'd left her. Water pooled on the floor around her feet. Our gazes met, and she shivered.

"Hey. You okay?" I dropped her bag and hurried over to wrap her in my arms.

"Cold. So very cold."

"Here's an idea. Go take a hot shower. I'll find some warm clothes for you and stoke the fire back to life. Sound good?"

She nodded but didn't move.

"Problem?" I asked.

She nodded again. "Your plan sounds like a winner. The only problem?" She leaned back until she could look into my face. "I have no idea where a shower might be located in this place."

I grinned. I studied her full lips and fought the compulsion to kiss her, strip her, and take her on the floor...or the counter...or the table...basically any way I could have her. "I see how that might be a problem." I forced my feet to move backwards. "Come on. The house isn't that big. I'll show you where the bathroom is. In the meantime, I'll find something for you to wear."

And it might be best if I wrapped her in layers and layers of flannel to keep me in check.

My grandparents' house was older, but they'd done a good job keeping it up to date, though not to the point of having a luxurious walk-in shower. The shower was a tub-slash-shower combo with a curtain that I'd grown up using. I was sure it would be an affront to what she was accustomed to.

I opened the door and said, "I'm sure this isn't as fancy as you're used to, but my grands were simple ranchers, who didn't need tiled walk-in showers."

She looked at me with a sigh. "I don't know why you do that, but we will talk about it later."

With a gentle shove on my chest to move me back, she shut me out of the room. "Find me something warm," she hollered through the paneled door.

I'd known a lot of women in the ten years we'd been apart. I confess that I'd slept with probably too many of them. However, in all that time, through all those dates, all the late nights drinking beer, I'd never enjoyed myself as much as I just did getting pushed around by Mae McCool.

The family had left winter clothes here over the past years. Mae wasn't as tall and thin as my sister, but trust me when I say I preferred women with curves. I'd been with women who were thin as a rail and never ate a bite of anything but dry salads. I never found any of them particularly attractive. They were like dating a clothes hanger... clothing looked better hanging on the frame than the frame itself.

Drawer and closet searches of my mother's and grandmother's clothes turned up plenty of socks, jeans, large shirts and even a pair of boots I thought would fit. I didn't know what she'd brought to sleep in while at the hotel, but I doubted the material was thick enough to provide the warmth she needed. I got her a pair of my drawstring pajama bottoms and a thermal shirt. With a thick pair of socks, she'd be protected from the chill but not from me. I could never forget the body under those clothes, regardless of how many layers there might be.

The water was still running when I knocked on the door. "Your evening wear, my lady," I said through the opening when I cracked the door.

Fuck. That was a mistake.

Steam filled the small room. The shower curtain, which had always seemed adequate, had stuck to her ass when she bent over to wash. Hell, I don't know why she was bent at the waist. Didn't care, either. All I cared about were those two glorious mounds of flesh clearly seen through the thin material. I adjusted myself in my jeans, which were suddenly a couple of sizes too small.

"Damn, Mae. Sorry."

She stood, removing my visual aid. Damn, again.

Her head poked around the edge of the curtain. "Sorry for what? Am I taking too long? Using up all the hot water? I bet you wanted to shower, too. Oops. Bad Mae." She grinned.

What she didn't realize was that her breasts were now plastered against the thin plastic, and I got an eyeful of nipple. She might not have noticed, but my cock jacked up to painful levels. I was pretty sure I'd be wearing a zipper indentation to bed tonight.

"No, no. You're fine. I had my shower." I held up my pajama bottoms and thermal shirt. "I'll just leave these right inside the door."

Bringing her here, being alone with her, was a mistake on my part, not that I really had a choice. Leaving her alone in the airport overnight hadn't been an option. But I had to get her gone. I hated my emotional vulnerability when I was around her. And she was the only woman who had the power to make me feel like that.

The kiss four weeks ago had haunted me night after night. Like a chump, I'd called her office a couple of times. However, she'd always been unavailable or out of town.

If I had her again, held her in my arms, took her like I dreamed of, I didn't think one night would be enough. I would need nights, maybe years, to work her out of my system.

No, I'd promised I'd keep my hands to myself, and that's what I was going to do, even if it killed me.

And it just might.

Chapter 8

~

Mae

~

The hot shower was a manna from heaven. The first blast of warm water had felt like pin pricks when it initially hit my toes, or rather my ten little chunks of ice. Don't get me wrong. Not only did Texas get winter weather, but my family had a condo in Colorado for our many snow ski vacations. However, I'd always been appropriately layered and never pranced through ice and snow in a pair of designer Jimmy Choo shoes, which were probably ruined after tonight.

After Michael had walked out of the airport to retrieve his ride, I'd gotten mad. Mad at the weather. Mad at how helpless I felt. Mostly, however, I was mad at myself for being so ill-prepared. I knew what

December in Montana could mean. I'd convinced myself that I'd be in and out of the state quickly, with barely any time to experience the weather, what with going from heated airport limo, to heated hotel, to heated conference room in the hotel, to another heated limo and then fly home. I told myself that those oh-so-brief exposures to the cold would be so fleeting that I wouldn't need a heavy coat.

As I turned my back to the scalding water to wash my hair, I gave myself a mental slap and made a solemn vow to do better in the future.

My libido laughed.

If I could find myself snowed in, sharing a house with just Michael Rockland, I was pretty sure I'd forget to even pack a bag on my next trip, or if there was a bag, it would only be filled with sexy lingerie.

And a heavy coat, my lawyer mind, my rational side, kicked in.

"Damn, Mae. Sorry,"

I straightened from where I'd been washing my toes, the inexpensive shower curtain plastered to my butt. That must have been a frightening vision.

Using the curtain to cover my nakedness, I peeked around the edge. Michael stood there, looking sexier than any man had a right to. I swear, male pheromones flooded the room. My lady parts had been frozen, but not dead earlier. Now that blood was flooding again, most of it rushed to swell my breasts and engorge my pelvis. Where was a shower massager when I needed it most?

"Sorry for what? Am I taking too long? Using up all the hot water? I bet you wanted to shower too. Oops. Bad Mae." I arched an eyebrow with a smile. If only Bad Mae were in charge. She would have invited him to join her. Sadly, Rational Mae had control at the moment, but Bad Mae had already begun plans to rope and gag Rational Mae tonight.

He set some clothing on the floor and closed the door.

As I finished showering, I thought about the night ahead. I was still a little peeved he'd never called for dinner like he'd suggested. Of course, in this day and age, I could have called him just as easily, I supposed. But I hadn't, and I knew why. He'd been the one to leave me ten years ago, and now he needed to do the pursuing, not me.

I dried off and pulled on the tie pants, sans panties. Either he hadn't wanted to go through my small carryon for them or he'd forgotten, or maybe he'd deliberately not brought me underwear. No matter to me. I usually slept in the nude anyway.

The sleeves of the thermal shirt covered my hands. I shoved the material up to my elbows, collected my clothes and wandered back to the living room where I found him sitting in a rocking chair in front of a roaring fire. My soul sighed at the homey vision.

"Hey there," I said.

He jerked around and smiled. "Better?"

"Much. Thank you."

With a nod, he gestured toward the fire. "I remembered how much you liked these."

Liked was such a weak word. Loved was more like it.

Even as a child, the dancing flames and crackle of wood burning soothed my soul like water did for others. When I'd been about three or so, and after every other trick to get me to bed failed, my parents had installed a fake burning fireplace. Those gyrating flames with their accompanying realistic sounds—or at least they had sounded real to three-year-old me— and no heat production to make my room sweltering, and I was hooked.

"I do love a fire. Thanks." I set my folded clothes in a chair by the door and joined him at the hearth. "Like my outfit?" I twirled like a model on a runway.

He grinned. His eyes twinkled. That could have been the reflections from the fire, but mentally, I went with twinkled because it sounded so much sexier in my head than reflected the flames.

"I don't believe my clothes ever looked that good on me."

I shook my head with a quiet snort and pulled up a rocker beside him. Both of us in rocking chairs in front of a roaring fire, dressed in pajama sleep pants and thick socks. The entire scene was almost too domesticated, as though we'd been a couple for decades instead of only speaking twice in the last ten years.

How could I still miss a guy who'd broken my heart twice? Once, ten years ago, and again four weeks ago when he hadn't called like he'd said. I wondered if I should bring it up.

We rocked for a couple of silent minutes.

"This is nice," he said. "Peaceful."

"Uh-huh." I took a deep breath and asked, "Why didn't you call after dinner at Maude's?"

He stared into the fire and didn't look at me. My

breath held, and my stomach rocked. I should have probably let sleeping dogs lie.

Finally, he turned to look at me. "I did call. More than once."

My mouth fell. "You did? Why... I mean, I don't understand."

With a shrug, he said, "Didn't have your cell phone number. You don't have a house phone listed, so I called your office. Couldn't get past your secretary. After the third brush-off, I assumed you told her not to put my calls through, and I gave up." A sad smile lifted the corners of his mouth. "It's fine. I understand."

"Wait. What do you understand? And for the record, I did not tell my assistant to block your calls. Why didn't you ask for my cell number?"

"I did. She said it was private."

I dropped my head to the back of the rocker and groaned. "I swear. She's a great assistant, and after all the media calls we got, um, earlier in the fall, I guess she thought she was helping. Probably thought you were someone out to cause me trouble."

The grin that lit his face was positively intoxicating. "Me? Give you trouble?" His hand pressed to his chest. "I'm crushed."

I scrunched my nose. "Sorry. She's a little overprotective since, well, she thought she was doing what I wanted."

"You could have called me," he said, arching a brow.

"Maybe, but I'd already stuck my neck out showing up at Maude's and asking her to call you. I told myself that if you wanted to hear from me again, you'd be in touch." I reached over and put my fingers on his forearm. "For the record, I don't discuss my private life with my assistant. She wouldn't have recognized your name, so I guess her not letting your call through is on me."

When I started to pull back my hand, he caught my fingers and held. He didn't say anything, just held on to my hand like it was a lifeline.

Now, I was just completely confused. My emotions were all over the place. My libido was making lewd and filthy, if interesting, suggestions. The rational lobe in my brain was flashing red lights and caution warnings, telling me to slow down and reminding me how much I'd been hurt in the past.

I wanted to pull back my hand out of self-preservation. I wanted to continue touching him out of, well, I didn't want to even think...love. I mean, how could I possibly still be in love with him? Sure, I probably still loved the boy I'd known ten years ago, but people change, right? The man wasn't the boy, right? It'd be insane to even think about sleeping with him, *right?*

A shiver racked my body at the thought of being naked with him, touching him, kissing him.

"You still cold?"

He reached behind the chair to snag a blanket off the sofa before I had time to say anything. I expected him to bundle me in the heavy material, maybe even tucking the edges around me. To my surprise, that wasn't what he did. Instead, he stood, moved his chair back, and spread the blanket in front of the hearth. He held out his hand, and when I took it, he pulled me to standing, pushed my chair backwards and then sat, lowering me with him. He put his arm around my shoulders and snuggled me tight against his body, which felt like hugging a furnace.

"Better?"

I wiggled a little to get settled in and sighed. "Much."

After a couple of minutes of quiet, I turned to look at him. "Question," I said.

"Answer," he replied.

I chuckled. "No, I have a question."

"Shoot."

I started to ask him about his sometime references to my money, or rather, my family's money, but I was warm, and comfortable pressed up next to him, and the fire was dancing and throwing off heat and shadows. If there was a heaven on earth, I was sitting in it.

So, I changed the question.

"Would you think I'm nuts if I wanted to sleep right here?"

He pressed his lips to the soft spot behind my ear that always made me moan. "Right here, meaning in my arms, or right here, meaning in front of the fire?" His whisper in my ear sent goose bumps popping up everywhere. "Because I'm thinking in front of the fire with you in my arms is the answer to every question."

My eyes shut as a heavy dose of longing shot from my belly to my groin. My heart raced. I knew if we slept together, we'd make love. I wanted to, even if my staunch rational side reminded me that I might regret it in the morning.

I might, but I knew without a doubt I would regret not taking advantage of this time. We could go home and back to our lives...our individual lives. I didn't know much about his, but there was one thing I had to be sure of...

"Is there someone waiting for you back home?" I asked. "You would have told me if you were married, I know, but maybe a girlfriend...someone who believes herself to be in love with you and you in love with her?"

He froze like a statue, and then asked, "Do you think I would be here, holding you like this, wanting you so badly my teeth ache if there was someone waiting for me in Texas?"

"I don't think so, but men—"

"Not this man," he said sharply. His posture eased as he wrapped more of himself around me. "Not all men are asshole jerks. I know that your recent past might suggest otherwise, but there are some men who are honest and faithful."

My recent past. I stilled in his arms. I hadn't given much thought to him knowing about my being humiliated by Roy, but, of course, he knew. Anyone with a newspaper or access to internet social media knew.

I gulped in air and prepared to fight the dragon. "You know about my non-wedding then?"

"Yes."

I nodded. "Newspaper or internet?"

His jaw tightened. "Neither. I was there."

My heart fell into my belly. He'd personally witnessed the worst day of my life. Did all this TLC from him spring from that? Was it possible he felt sorry for me and thought he was helping by being all emo and caring?

"I can hear the firing of ideas in that brain of yours," he said as he brushed my long hair off my neck. "You're wondering who invited me, and my answer is nobody invited me. I crashed your wedding."

"Why?" I whispered.

He sighed, the warm breath along the nape of my neck raising more goose bumps. "I had to see for myself—you married to someone else. I needed, or thought I needed, the concrete fact that you had found happiness with someone other than me."

I scoffed. "Well, that's not exactly what happened."

He hugged me. "I noticed."

I needed to know, so I asked. "Did you think of me over the past ten years? Wonder how I was doing? What I was doing?"

"Every day," he said quietly.

I closed my eyes. "Then why didn't you contact me?"

"Thought about it, but I didn't know if you wanted to hear from me. Maybe I was just a bad memory, or someone you forgot about a long time ago."

"No," I whispered. "Not someone I forgot." I looked at him over my shoulder. "You're kind of hard to forget."

He gave me a crooked smile, and everything inside me lit up like a marquee.

I didn't say anything else. It didn't matter what he thought about my money, my family, or even my upbringing. I wanted to keep tonight in the here and now and not build fantasies about the future.

"I have an idea," he said.

"Yeah? What's that?"

"I want to surprise you. Can you move the rocking

chairs over to the wall along with the coffee table behind us?"

I raised both eyebrows. "Okay..." I dragged out the word.

We stood, and he walked out of the room. I got busy moving furniture pretty sure I knew what he was up to. I wasn't surprised when he struggled through the doorway with a mattress.

I hurried across the room. "Let me help."

"I've got it. Just make sure I don't break the lamp or something."

"Okay, if you're sure I can't help carry it."

"I'm sure," he said, then grunted as he flipped it sideways to get it through the doorframe.

I rushed to move additional items and furniture out of his way as he staggered forward. He only knocked over a magazine rack and the fireplace tools. I considered that a win.

"Now you can help me," he said. "Grab one end, and we'll set this on the floor."

We got the heavy double mattress with its fitted sheet settled, and then he said, "Be right back."

He headed back to where he'd come from and returned with two pillows, a top sheet and a blanket.

"You think we'll need that blanket?" I asked, fully intending to use his body heat to keep me warm. Even the thought made my temperature jump ten degrees.

He grinned, and my insides melted.

"Probably not, but better safe than sorry."

After tossing the pillows down and spreading out the top sheet and blanket, he waved his hand over the makeshift bed. "This work?"

"More than you know," I said, suddenly nervous.

I sat on the side of the mattress facing the fire, my heart jumping around in my chest. He sat at my back, put his arm around my hips, and rested his hand on the mattress by my side. My back heated when he pressed his chest to it. My lungs seized.

Brushing my hair over my shoulder, he said, "Nothing has to happen tonight if you don't want it to."

His quiet voice in my ear made me shiver even as disappointment flooded my belly. "It doesn't?" I whispered. I wasn't whispering because I was trying to make my voice sexy. I'd lost my breath when he sat so near. "But what if I want something to happen?"

Chapter 9

~

Rock

~

I was serious when I said nothing had to happen. I've never forced myself on a woman, and I never would. However, the woman in my arms tonight wasn't just another female. She was my fantasy, the woman I compared every other woman to. None had ever come close.

I'd always known Mae wasn't perfect, but she was perfect for me.

And now, she'd just told me that she wanted something to happen tonight.

My cock, already awake and at half-mast since seeing her at the airport, shoved against the flannel pajama pants I wore.

But I also realized she was exhausted. I knew how

drained I felt when I was outside in the cold and then came inside to warm up. I was still battling my thoughts when she turned slightly and placed her hand on my cheek. I regretted not shaving before I went to the airport, but I'd been expecting my family, not the love of my life.

I put my fingers over hers and pulled her hand to my mouth, pressing a kiss in her palm. Her pupils enlarged, and her eyes darkened. Leaning forward, she kissed me, her other hand sliding around my neck and her fingers threading into my hair. I licked her lower lip, and she opened her mouth and flicked out her tongue to meet mine.

Desire ricocheted through my chest and spread from head to toe. I jerked her to me and deepened the kiss, thrusting my tongue into her mouth. She moaned and stroked her tongue along the side of mine.

Turning slightly, I lowered her to the mattress and followed her down. Her legs wrapped around my calves, her fingers running lines down my neck and onto my shoulders.

"Babe," I said with a whisper. "I want you so bad."

She wiggled her groin against my engorged dick, and as impossible as it seemed, more blood filled its veins.

"I noticed," she said with another wiggle.

I groaned. "You're killing me."

I grabbed the hem of my thermal shirt and pulled it over her head. My heart might have stopped beating momentarily. The flickering light from the fire danced over her perfect breasts. Her nipples jutted outward, and my mouth salivated for a taste. I leaned downed and covered one breast with my mouth while my thumb and forefinger rolled the other nipple. She tasted like heaven. She looked like an angel fallen down just for me.

Her fingers tugged at my shirt until I pulled away long enough to whip it over my head and toss it away. Her nails raked my back as she continued to grind against me.

I untied her pants and ran my hand between her legs. She was wet and hot against my hand. I slipped two fingers inside her, and her hips lifted off the mattress. Moaning, she rolled her head side to side and humped my fingers. Pressing my thumb into her rigid nub, I said, "Let go. I want to watch you climax all over my hand."

Biting her bottom lip, she groaned and her thrusts against my hand became harder. And then she was there, crying out my name while she contracted and squeezed my fingers. Pink flushed her chest as she continued to groan.

When it was over, I pulled my fingers from her. I was beyond aroused to the point of pain, but I didn't want to force the sex issue if she was ready to stop.

As I moved away, she grabbed my arm. "Where are you going?"

"Nowhere, if you don't want me to."

"I want you somewhere, all right. I want you between my legs, and I mean now, mister."

I chuckled, from her words and my relief. I pulled a condom from the pocket of my pajama pants and put it on. I was inside her in the next move.

I thought my heart was going to explode from the degree of love that filled it.

I brought her to a second climax before finding my own release, a release that was ten years in the making.

There'd been other women, but there'd never been another Mae McCool, and I didn't think I'd ever find this kind of bliss again.

I woke early because my internal clock was still on Central Time, or that's what I told myself. It could have been the vanilla scent from Mae's hair tickling my nose. It could have been the rarity of waking up with a woman in my arms. Staying the night after sex wasn't my usual style. After I'd given up Mae, I'd given up on finding the special connection I saw between my parents...until last night. Ten years without her, and then wham. She was back in my life, and I felt like I'd plugged in the last piece of a puzzle and could finally see the whole picture.

The thought that, for her, this might be rebound sex crossed my mind. I tried to ignore it, but she had been through a horrific public breakup not that long ago. That she would still be affected by that event would only make sense. We would need to talk about it, but I'd put it off as long as I could. I was too comfortable at the moment to rock the boat. I shut my eyes and let her essence fill my senses.

Sleet pinged on the windows. The sun had barely begun to rise. The fire had burned down to one fat log and a pile of embers. I was on my side, the sexy curves of Mae's body pressed to mine. My morning wood appreciated her soft flesh and rose to salute it.

Slowly, I pulled my numb arm from under her neck. She sniffled and adjusted her position, not waking. I slipped off the mattress and stood. The blanket rested in a heap on the floor near her feet. The white top sheet draped across her hip, leaving the soft flesh of her back exposed to the now chilly room. My heart swelled in my chest as I watched her side rise and fall with her breaths. The action of moving my arm had spread her long blonde hair over my pillow. I'd never seen a more beautiful woman, and I doubted I could ever love a woman more than at this minute.

I watched her sleep for more minutes than I would ever admit. Because, if this turned out to be a one and done, I needed to store all the memories I could. Remembering her, remembering last night, would get me through even the darkest times.

I pulled on my pajama bottoms and shoved my feet into a pair of boots. After wrestling a thick jacket over my bare torso, I headed to the front porch. Without thinking yesterday, I'd left the leather work gloves I used to haul wood on the seat of the swing outside. I wiggled my fingers into the stiff leather, more than a little irritated at myself. I trudged around the corner of the house to the cord of seasoned wood piled there. The frozen snow crunched under my boots. My breath shot steamy fog from my mouth, and my nose ran in the cold wind.

Grabbing as many logs as I could carry in one load, I brought them back to the porch and piled them there. Since I was already miserable, I headed back to the pile and carried back a second load. This should keep the fire going for a while.

I could've turned up the thermostat, but where was the fun in that?

After stoking the fire back to life, I added some

fresh wood to the flame. Behind me, I felt movement, and I turned. Mae stretched her arms over her head with the smile of a happy woman, or at least that was my interpretation.

"Morning," I said.

"Morning." She covered her mouth as she yawned. "What time is it?"

"Six."

Her eyes shifted as she did the time conversion in her head. "Seven at home, then."

"Right. Coffee?"

"Oh, God, yes, please."

I grinned. "When you said that last night, you weren't talking about coffee."

"Michael!" She ducked her head under the covers.

I laughed as I dropped onto the mattress beside her. Pulling the sheet off her head, I wrapped my arms around her and pulled her to me. I kissed her. "Good morning."

She pulled back. "No. I have morning breath."

She did, but I said, "I love morning breath," and kissed her again.

This time she kissed me back, and our two morning breaths mingled until nothing mattered but making love to her again.

Chapter 10

~

Mae

~

He didn't have morning breath. That was so unfair. I was sure my breath was akin to sniffing a camel hump after a day of giving rides. His was cold and crisp, like outside air. His lips were like kissing a glacier. His tongue was definitely warmer. But whew. As Michael's tongue stroked mine, all thoughts of my breath flew out of my mind. I didn't care about anything but getting him naked again.

"Take that coat off," I demanded. "Where have you been keeping it? In the freezer?"

He grinned as he jerked it off, along with kicking off his boots and pants.

"Better?"

I snuggled against him and hissed. "Yikes. You're

freezing. I'm going to start calling you Frosty the Snowman. All you need is a carrot nose and a top hat."

He rubbed his ice-cold chest against mine. "I know. I decided I'll keep you hostage here through the winter and use you like my personal heater." Then he tangled his legs with mine as I laughed.

"Don't you think we'll be missed if neither of us return to Texas and our jobs?" Somehow, the idea didn't freak me out as much as it should have.

Brushing his frosty nose—um, it felt more like his carrot was a little lower than his face!—against mine, he said, "Who cares?"

And for once, my job shot to the back of my mind.

I rolled him under me and stretched out along his firm body. Face to face, my toes were at his ankles, but the most significant parts lined up perfectly. Mouth to mouth. His hard chest cushioning my boobs. Our bellies rising and falling together. And finally, ideal alignment of my soft, willing sex with his long, rock-hard cock.

"Now, this is better," he said, and raised his head to kiss me.

"Much," I agreed, and wiggled a little to make sure he was interested.

If the granite dick jabbing into my stomach was any indication, I had his attention.

"Careful with the merchandise," he said with a grin. "You break it, you bought it."

I kissed his lips then began leaving a trail of kisses down his neck to his chest. He groaned when I circled the tip of my tongue around his nipple and bit down. His cock jumped and slammed against my ribs.

Continuing my journey downward, I left licks and nibbles and kisses all along the way, until my tongue slid across the slit in the head of his dick. He groaned, and his hips jutted upward with that one lick.

I crawled between his thighs and kissed the inside of each one. His fingers found my head and threaded into my hair. I pulled back and said, "Hold on, cowboy. I've still got some playing to do."

He shoved both pillows and the blanket under his head, elevating him until he was looking down at me.

I smiled up at him. "Like to watch, huh?"

"Mae, I'm a guy. Of course, I want to watch someone give me head, but honey, you don't have to."

I hadn't last night. Every cell in my body had been consumed with getting him inside of me. I hadn't wanted foreplay, or any delay, before I could feel him gliding into me again. Even as I thought about last night, my pelvis engorged with arousal.

Salty fluid hit my tongue with my second lick. Above my head, Michael hissed and sucked in his stomach.

"But I want to," I said and took the tip into my mouth. I sucked and licked around the head before running the flat of my tongue down the throbbing vein on the underside. His fingers tightened in my hair as he blew out a long breath. I licked my way down to his balls and carefully sucked each one into my mouth for a kiss before nibbling my way back up to the head. There, I took him deep into my mouth.

His thighs quivered, and I smiled to myself. I loved having him under my control.

"Fuck. That's enough," he said and jerked me up his body. "Ride me, babe."

Throwing back my hair, I lowered myself onto his rigid cock, and he groaned.

"Wait." He lifted me off him like I weighed nothing, and then rolled to his side to grab a condom from last night's stash.

"Now." Grabbing my waist, he rolled me under him and thrust deep, his balls slapping me with every plunge.

I wrapped my legs around his waist. He slid his hands under my ass and lifted me until my hips were off the bed and he was hitting a special spot inside me with every stroke.

My heart hammered violently in my ears. My breaths came in choppy starts and stops. As he continued to screw me, tension like a tightly wound coil curled inside me.

"Don't stop," I moaned. "Please."

"Never, babe. Never." He leaned over and kissed me as the coil inside released, shooting electricity and sparks through my system. A couple of thrusts, and he held tight to me as he found his own release.

"Wow," I was able to say through gasps. "Merry Christmas to me."

He chuckled. "Merry Christmas Eve. Christmas is tomorrow."

"True. But I think I just got my present for this year."

He kissed me and rolled off. I missed the feel of his weight bearing down on me. Missed the furnace-like heat he produced.

"I'm going to grab a quick shower," I announced. I knew if I stayed where I was, I'd never go back to Texas. I needed to call the airport from the bathroom and check the flight schedules. Maybe I could find something for later in the day. Or better, maybe the airport was still closed. I crossed my fingers at that idea.

I turned the water on in the sink before I dialed my airline about rebooking a flight back to Texas. So stupid, but I didn't want him hearing me ask about leaving.

And my prayers were not answered.

The airport would open at ten and, according to the airlines, would be back to full service by noon. If wanted, I could rebook my flight from yesterday and fly out at two that afternoon.

I did not want.

I thanked the woman answering the call and hung up. As I washed my hair, I tried to decide exactly what I was going to tell Michael.

One option was lying. I could tell him everything was still closed, but then how would I explain his parents' arrival?

Another option was not to mention the airport. If he wanted me gone, wouldn't he have called the airport while I was in the shower and checked?

Last option was the truth. Tell him I didn't want to go, that I wanted to stay here for Christmas. But that wasn't really a viable option. After my history with both Michael and Roy, I had trouble trusting people with any information that might give them something to hold over my head.

Still, I didn't have any reason to rush home. My folks were gone on their big trip and were supposed to be in France for Christmas. Of course, I had invitations to join my uncle and aunt and their family, and I knew I'd be welcomed with open arms, but I couldn't get past the idea they might still feel sorry for me because of Roy's ridiculous public proclamation.

Plus, it would be only Risa, her husband, and their new daughter, not Wendy. The last time I'd spoken with Risa, she'd told me that Wendy had gone on an extended leave of absence. No one knew if she would be home for Christmas. That little piece of news had me blowing a gasket. Roy hadn't simply screwed up my life. He'd embarrassed my cousin, too.

As I stepped from the shower, it dawned on me that I had nothing clean to wear except panties. Michael might enjoy that, but I was fairly certain I'd be a tad chilly.

I slipped on my underwear, wrapped a towel around me—which barely met in the front—and opened the door. I was met by a long wolf whistle.

"I'm liking your idea," he said and reached for me.

"Stay back," I growled threateningly, or I tried to. I think my giggle gave me away.

He wrapped his arms around me and turned me until my rear was braced on the back of the sofa. Then he came in for a long, wet kiss that sent sparks of lust dancing along my spine.

I gave his shoulder a push, not that I had the strength to physically push him away. Still, he took a step back, a very short step.

"I need clothes," I said. "This isn't the Caribbean, and there is no nude beach that I can stretch out on for a tan."

He pumped his brows. "I know a place you can stretch out."

I laughed and pushed at him again. "Surely there's

something near here where I can get some winter clothes. A Walmart or something?"

"So, you're staying?" he asked.

"Right. I forgot to mention that the airport is still iced in." I shrugged and tried to look annoyed. "So, you're stuck with me for another day."

Then I remembered his parents. Damn. What if they flew in today?

"Your folks. Have you talked to them? What are they being told about flying?"

"Called 'em while you were in the shower. They aren't coming until the day after Christmas. Did you know today is one of the busiest, if not *the* busiest, day for airlines? There was no way for them to get a flight, even if the airport opened, so no company for a couple of days."

One bullet dodged.

I grimaced. "Did you tell them I was here?"

"I might have mentioned an airport rescue."

I dropped my head and pressed my face into his chest...not that I could make any kind of indention in that slab of hard muscles. "How embarrassing."

"No reason to be upset. They didn't mind that you were using one of the guest rooms."

Lifting my head and rolling my eyes up to meet his gaze, I gave him a smile of total relief. "Thank you for that. Now, clothes? And is there food? I'm starving."

Food wasn't an issue as he'd already filled the kitchen in preparation for his family. For clothes, he'd search through his mom and grandmom's clothes and had enough to get me through a couple of days. Of course, that meant I'd be washing underwear every night, or going commando. If I could get over the idea of my hooha freezing, the commando thought wasn't nearly as frightening as I thought it would be.

As soon as breakfast was over, Michael announced, "Get dressed. We're headed to the woods."

I looked at him with a raised eyebrow. "Excuse me? Why?"

"My folks expect me to have this place decorated when they get here. Family tradition is to cut a tree from the woods. Grandpa began planting blue spruce trees when dad was born, and he planted one every year on Dad's birthday. We've got quite a few to pick from."

I stared at him with what I hoped he recognized as incredulity. "Cut down a tree? Are you kidding me?"

"You've never cut down a tree for Christmas, have you?"

I sniffed. "Mom's decorator did our trees."

He blinked and shook his head. "Wait. Are you saying you've never hung ornaments or lights or anything?"

Heat flushed up my neck, and I knew I sounded like a poor, little rich girl.

He laughed. "Honey, have I got things to show you."

I pumped my eyebrows. "I think you've already shown me your things."

That just made him laugh louder, and he pulled me close for a hug.

Two hours later, I staggered through the back door hugging the prickly branches of a green monster. Michael had set up a tree stand before we left and, now we struggled to get the massive tree trunk situated between silver bolts and get it upright and stable.

Once the tree stood on its own, he handed me a couple of boxes. "Ornaments," he said as a way of explanation.

"Okay," I replied. I meant to sound like I knew what to do, but obviously he saw through that.

"Hang them on the tree after I get the lights on."

I hung balls, angels, bells, icicles, and a few stars. The whole time, my nose was treated to the fresh scent of spruce. I saw no reason to hang ornaments on the back of the tree since no one would ever see them, but he was a Christmas tree expert, or that's what he said. Christmas trees must have balls, tinsel and lights on *all* sides, even the ones facing the wall.

We finally flopped on the couch in the middle of the afternoon to inspect our work. One fully decorated Christmas tree, some greenery over the hearth, and a light-up Santa watching us from the corner.

Having Santa hover there felt a little strange. Sort of like an adult version of Elf-on-a-Shelf. I thought I might have to throw a towel over Santa's head if we got a little frisky on the sofa. He looked a little judgmental just standing there.

Chapter 11

Rock

I put my arm around Mae. She leaned against me. My heart, and other areas of my body, swelled in response. She sighed.

"Everything okay?" I asked.

"Perfect. Why?"

"That was a heavy sigh."

She snuggled in under my arm. "That was a sigh of total contentment."

I smiled. "Good."

"The house smells so good. I love the aroma of fresh cut spruce, don't you?"

"One of the best things about Christmas is all the great smells. I've got an idea."

"Oh?" She chuckled. "You've had a couple of really great ideas last night."

I laughed. "Well, when it comes to you, I always have those ideas, but this one is something different."

"What's that?" She turned her head to look up at me.

"There's a small town about an hour from here that goes all out for the holidays. Let's drive up there and see the Christmas lights. Maybe even do a little ice skating. Heck, maybe you can even sit on Santa's lap."

"Think things will still be open? It's Christmas Eve."

"Last year, everything was open until about ten or eleven, so sure. We have plenty of time."

She shrugged. "Sounds like fun. Let's do it."

"Layer up, and let's head out."

By the time we reached Winter Springs, Montana, it was close to five in the evening. The streets were still alive with families drinking hot chocolate, skating on the ice rink in the middle of town, and last-minute shoppers scurrying from store to store.

"Michael," Mae said, laying her hand on my arm. "This is like something out of a movie."

I smiled, pleased she was as taken with the town as I had always been. "Agreed. Let me find a place to park, and then let's walk the square."

Her face was bright with a smile and eyes that seemed to dance. As soon as I parked, she jumped from the truck, ready to explore all the little town had to offer.

I took her gloved hand, and we started toward the

town square, the frozen snow crunching under our boots.

"So, where to first?" I asked. "Shopping? Dinner? Skating?"

"You are such a guy," she said with a laugh. "Shopping, of course."

Bemused, I agreed. "Of course."

"No, seriously," she said. "I was going to do my shopping when I got back from Montana. I haven't bought a thing for my family or my assistant."

"No problem. Lead on." I would happily follow this woman anywhere.

Five shops later, my hands were full of sacks of wrapped presents, and the top one was teetering. "I'm pretty sure I can't carry another thing," I said.

"But I'm not done," she said, with a slight whine.

"I'll take these to the truck and catch back up with you."

She smiled and kissed me lightly on the lips. "Thank you."

I headed off to Grandpop's truck with one thought...this was how it should be. Mae and me together. It didn't matter what the activity was or what the day would bring, I'd never been surer that we belonged together. But I couldn't get a bead on her. Did she feel the same? Did she see us together for the long-term, or was this just a vacation from her real life? I didn't know and I wasn't sure how to go about getting the answers to all my unvoiced questions.

While I looked for her in shops, I did a little Christmas shopping of my own. After all, tomorrow was Christmas, and I wanted to have something to give Mae.

When I finally found her, five additional shopping bags dangled from her wrists.

"Are you kidding me?" I joked. "Did you leave anything for other people to buy?"

She stuck out her tongue, and then laughed. "I love Christmas, and yes, I know I go overboard with gifts." She shrugged. "Always have and probably always will."

"Want me to take those back to the truck?"

Shaking her head, she said, "I've got them. Where to next?"

"Ice skating?" I asked. I hoped she'd say no. It'd been years since I'd been on skates, and I was fairly sure I would make a fool out of myself.

"Let's don't and say we did." She grinned. "Seriously, I can ice skate; I just don't enjoy it." She gestured toward her feet. "Weak ankles."

"Whew," I said with a long breath. "I didn't want to make a fool out of myself."

She laughed and linked her arm through mine. "This town is wonderful."

We began walking and window shopping. The town held an annual window decorating contest, so every window display focused on some aspect of Christmas. Lots of snow scenes. A few church-related ones. One window showed a cute couple holding hands while ice skating. We were nearing the end of the block when snow began floating down from the clouds, completing the perfect night.

Mae pulled me closer and pressed herself tight against my side. "Thank you. This is the best Christmas Eve I've had in a while. The stores. The snow. The families. I love it all."

"Me, too." Her included.

We crossed the street and headed toward the only stop we hadn't yet made. In front of us was Santa sitting in a massive chair. As we neared, he lifted the child off his lap and gave a mighty, "Ho, ho, ho, James. Merry Christmas."

The young child looked at Santa with wide eyes. "Bye, Santa." He ran toward the couple I assumed were his parents and began a long-winded story about everything he'd asked for. Santa's helper handed the couple a white folder, which they immediately opened and began oohing and awing over the picture inside.

"Want to talk to Santa?" I joked.

To my surprise, Mae answered, "I sure do." She handed me her sacks and hurried toward him.

I chuckled and followed behind. I had no idea who Santa was or what age he was, but his eyes lit up, and a wide smile formed on his lips when Mae sat on his knee. I've never hated Santa more.

Standing by Santa's photographer elf, I said, "Do get a good picture."

She chuckled. "Oh, I will. That's my husband. He looks a little too happy."

I snorted. "That's my girl, and I was thinking I might have to kill or maim him." So maybe Mae wasn't technically my girl, but I was going to rectify that as quickly as I could.

She giggled. "I guess we have to give him a break. It's been a long day." She looked at me. "Go join them and let me get a shot of all of you." She leaned toward me. "I already have a picture of the two of them that will get me on that cruise I've been waiting to take."

As I walked inside the fence to join Santa and Mae, Santa whispered something into her ear. Mae's face pinkened, and she shrugged.

"Okay, I've sent her man to keep you in line, Mr. Santa," his wife called. "Let's get all of you into the picture."

I took a position beside and a little behind Mae, placing my hand on her shoulder. She looked back at me and smiled. I couldn't help but smile back.

"That's it, Santa," his wife called. "I've got the shot."

Mae stood. "Thank you, Santa."

He winked. "I think you'll get everything you asked for."

Santa's wife joined them and handed me a couple of folders. "The pictures are usually ten dollars each, but I'll give you both of them for fifteen dollars."

"Sold," I said, and pulled my wallet out to pay.

She took the money, and then said to Santa, "Looking forward to that Caribbean cruise."

He groaned.

Mae and I laughed, collected our sacks, and headed for the truck.

"Want to grab dinner?" I asked. "It'll save us from having to cook when we get home."

It was after seven-thirty and I knew that, by the time we got home and unpacked, it'd be too late to start cooking.

"Great idea," she said. "Pick the place."

By the time I parked the truck back at my grand-parents' house, it was after ten.

Mae groaned and rubbed her stomach. "I ate too much."

"I warned you that the buffalo steaks were good."

She opened her door. "You were right. I feel like I need to go for a long jog."

I laughed. "A little dark for that. Maybe tomorrow we can go cross-country skiing. That'll burn a few calories."

"Deal."

As I loaded up the sacks from the backseat, I asked, "Are all these presents?"

She shook her head. "There might be a few items for me."

"Sexy pajamas?" I pumped my eyebrows and leered.

She scoffed. "In these temperatures? Not hardly."

I groaned. "Damn. We're headed somewhere warm."

With a laugh, she said, "Trust me. Nothing exciting. Mostly clean undies and a couple of warm shirts."

With our arms loaded, we headed into the warm house and out of the bitter cold. Since we'd been sleeping in the living room, and she'd never been assigned a bedroom, she turned in a circle looking around. "I have no idea where to put all this."

I gestured toward a closed door. "In there will be fine. It's not like you'll be using that bed."

"Really?" She tossed me a saucy look, and put her hand on her cocked hip. "You think I'll just fall back on that mattress with you?"

I swept her off her feet, and she laughed loudly.

"Put me down," she said.

I carried her into the guest room. "Drop the bags," I growled, "or else."

She giggled and dropped the bags on the bed.

I turned around and walked out. When I was by the fireplace, I set her down on the mattress. Then, an unfamiliar insecurity flooded my gut. Had I over-played my hand? "This okay?" I asked. If she said she'd rather sleep alone tonight, I'd be disappointed, but it was her decision.

"Very okay." She pulled me down onto the mattress beside her. "As long as I'm not sleeping here alone."

I kissed her, lowering her back onto the mattress. I pulled my mouth away long enough to say, "Definitely not alone."

I woke up in the middle of the night thinking about food. It was Christmas, and I'd bought all the necessary foodstuff for my mom to prepare a feast for the family. Even though it was just Mae and me, I felt this need to make her Christmas as special as I could.

"Michael?" she said, her word slurring sleepily.

"Shhh. Go back to sleep. It's early."

She yawned. "What time is it? Why are you awake?"

"It's about four. I'm not awake. This is just a dream."

She snorted and scooted backwards. I wrapped my arms around her.

"Mae?"

"Yeah?"

"Do you know how to make cornbread dressing?"

"Nope. Cook always did that. Should I learn how?"

I kissed the top of her head. The scent of her vanilla and cinnamon shampoo swirled around my face. "Nope. You're perfect just the way you are."

"You are, too," she said with another yawn.

She dropped back to sleep quickly. I didn't. My mind became flooded with ways I could make her mine.

Finally, at a little after five, I slipped from the bed.

Chapter 12

Mae

The aroma of bacon tickled my senses. Before I could react, that delicious scent was replaced with the magnificence of fresh brewed coffee. My eyes popped open and beheld the most wondrous sight. A sexy man wearing only jeans, half-zipped, was handing me a cup of liquid gold.

"Give me," I croaked out.

He laughed and handed me the hot ceramic mug. "Merry Christmas, beautiful."

My heart sputtered. "Merry Christmas, handsome."

He grinned, and my jittering heart jumped and slammed into my chest. Waking up to that face and that smile had to be every woman's dream.

"Did I smell bacon?" I held up crossed fingers.

Smiling, he tilted his head. "You did. There's also going to be pancakes as soon as you get out of bed."

"But breakfast in bed..." I whined.

"I could do that," he agreed. "Except I fear the syrup would end up in places other than the pancakes."

I arched an eyebrow, or at least I tried. I hoped I didn't look surprised instead. "That does sound interesting, but another time." My stomach let out a loud growl.

"Damn, woman," he said. "Did we let a bear in here last night?"

I threw a pillow at him, which he caught without effort.

"Do I have time for a quick shower first?" I asked.

"Sure. I won't pour the pancakes until you're ready, but be warned. I've already eaten some of the bacon."

"I'll hurry." I slugged back some coffee and stood. "Five minutes."

"Right," he said with an eyeroll.

My phone trilled on the table, and I checked the caller ID and groaned. "Damn. Give me ten minutes instead."

"Merry Christmas," I said as a way of answering my phone. I went into the bathroom and closed the door behind me.

"*Feliz navidad*, Chicko. When did you get back from Montana?" KatiLyn asked me. "I thought you were going to call so we could finish the plans for the New Year's Eve bash at your place."

I winced because, one, I knew I was going to get

chewed out, and two, I'd totally forgotten about the New Year's Eve party.

"I'm still in Montana."

"What? Why?"

"Big snowstorm. The airport closed."

"I know. Saw it on the news, but didn't it reopen the next morning?"

"Did it?" I lied.

KatiLyn exhaled a long sigh. "What is going on?"

I huffed a breath. "Fine. I got snowed in and didn't have a hotel room, or anything warm to wear, and you'll never guess who I ran into..." I laughed nervously. "Michael Rockland. And he let me stay at his grandparents' place."

"Soooo, you're staying with Rock and his grand-parents?"

I cleared my throat. "Not exactly."

"Opal Mae McCool. You are the worst liar. There is no grandparents' place, and you're shacked up at some hotel with Michael Rockland, right?"

"No. There is a grandparents' place." I winced again. "It's just that Michael's dad inherited the farm when they died. His family was going to spend Christmas here, you know, like a holiday vacation."

"Was spending, as in they aren't now?"

"I couldn't get out, and they couldn't get in."

"But—"

"I know. I could have gone home the next day, but I didn't want to, so there."

My BFF was silent for a long moment before she released a long exhale. "Mae. You know I only want the best for you, but I'm worried. Rock broke your heart. Crushed it, actually. I've not forgotten the nights of weeping, the days of not eating, not going to classes, turning down date after date. For a while, I thought I'd lost you, but you fought your way back. You got over him. You moved on. Don't do this. Don't go backwards. This fall has been a total hell for you. Don't complicate things further by falling for him again."

I heard her, but everything inside me resisted her well-meaning advice. "He's changed," I protested. "It's not the same this time."

"I'm assuming this means you've slept with him."

I didn't reply.

"I don't want to see you hurt again," she repeated, her voice softer now.

"I won't be," I said. "Really. I've got all my emotions locked down tight. Threw away the key and everything. I'm just having a little Christmas fun. It was better than coming home to an empty condo."

"You should have called me. You wouldn't have been alone."

"And what? I could spend Christmas with you and your latest flame? No thank you."

"Be careful, Mae. Don't let him hurt you again. And don't fall in love with him again."

Too late.

"I hear ya. I'll think about everything you've said."

"Should I cancel the party for New Year's Eve? Or move it to my place?"

"No. I'll be home way before then. I promise."

"Be careful. Love ya. Merry Christmas."

"You too, KatiLyn."

I clicked off and started the water running in the shower, KatiLyn's words echoing around in my mind. She was right. It had been a hard year, capped off by the non-wedding of my nightmares. And then Dad turning over company operations to me, and yeah, maybe I wasn't thinking as clearly as I should. Finding Michael in Montana had been a shock. I was thankful that he'd been there for me, and the last couple of days had been wonderful, but snowed-in in Montana with him wasn't reality. Reality was Texas and work, not Montana and play. My BFF was right. I did need to go home and face reality.

As I was drying off, I realized I'd left my new underwear in the guest room in a sack. My mind really wasn't clicking on all cylinders. After wrapping the towel around me, I stepped into the living room to cross to the guest room. I stopped dead in my tracks.

"Mae! How nice to see you, dear," Michael's mother said.

I pulled the towel tight across my breasts. Gathering my wits, I managed not to squeak out my response. "Hello, Mrs. Rockland. Excuse me."

I dashed into the bedroom and closed the door. I was proud of myself for not fainting or slamming the door. What were Michael's parents doing here? Hadn't he said they'd be here after Christmas? Good lord. I prayed to have a heart attack and die or for the earth to open up and swallow me. Unfortunately, neither happened, and I would have to dress and face them.

As I finished buttoning my new flannel shirt, I remembered the mattress in front of the fireplace. Oh God, had I left any clothes on the floor? Would it not be obvious what had been going on? I swear, I was more embarrassed at this moment than I'd been telling five hundred people that Roy had left me at the altar.

There was a knock at the door. "Mae?" It was Michael, soon to be the *late* Michael Rockland.

"What?" I snapped in a whisper through the door.

"Can I come in?"

"No."

The doorknob turned, and Michael stepped in. He grimaced. "I'm sorry. They thought it would be fun to surprise me by coming early."

I whirled around and walked across the room. "Did they know I was here?"

When he didn't immediately reply, I turned to face him. "Michael? Did they know?"

He nodded, and then shook his head. "Sort of. Kind of."

"Which one is it? Sort of or kind of?"

He ran his fingers through his hair and looked away from me. "I told them you'd stayed that first night. I didn't mention that you hadn't flown out when the airport reopened."

My eyes shut in mortification. "You knew the airport reopened the next morning?"

"Yeah, but I didn't want you to go, so…"

"So, when I said it was still closed, you went along with it."

"I didn't want you to leave," he repeated.

"Well," I said with a forced chuckle. "I guess they gave themselves a surprise as well as you."

"It's okay," he said and stepped toward me. "We're adults. What we do is completely our business." He took my hand. "They understand that."

I snorted. "Sure, they do." I pulled my hand away

and stepped back. "They never liked me. This should cement their feelings."

He frowned. "What are you talking about? Of course, they liked you. It was you who was embarrassed to be seen with me. It was your parents who looked down on my family."

"What?" My mouth gaped. "They most certainly did not look down on your family or anyone else. And I was most certainly not embarrassed to be with you."

"Really? How many times did you invite me to your house? You don't need to think about it. I know. Once. I was in your house once. We were together for over six months, and you had me over once."

I shook my head. "No, that can't be right."

"Oh, it's right."

"Are you saying my parents were rude to you when you came over?"

"Oh no, they were polite enough, just like they were to your cook or the gardener. Your dad let me know that while it was fine that you had some fun with me that summer, he had bigger and better things planned for you than some guy from a lower middle-class family."

"He did not," I replied, or maybe I might have shouted. But I was furious. Even though my parents had money, they never looked down at anyone. They treated everyone with respect.

His eyes blazed. "I was there. You weren't."

"I think you're the one with the problem, not my folks. How many snide remarks about my upbringing and family have I let slide? Tons! You need to grow up and get over yourself."

He snorted. "Get over myself? How about you face a little reality when it comes to your parents?"

My mouth dropped open.

He held up a hand. "Don't say anything. I need to cool off." He left, slamming the door behind him.

I was sure steam poured out of my ears. My heart pounded painfully. My breaths were harsh and labored. I had never been so angry. How dare he lie about my parents like that? But hadn't all his veiled comments really shown his true feelings? I'd heard them and let them slide. Maybe I should have confronted him then.

My phone trilled. The caller ID read "Dad".

"Merry Christmas," I said as brightly as I could.

"Hi, honey. Merry Christmas to you, too," said Mom.

"Are you having fun? How's Paris?"

"Oh, Mae. It's the trip of my dreams. We're having so much fun."

"I'm so glad." And I was. She deserved this trip.

"Have you got big plans for today? Are you headed over to Risa and Trevor's? I know you want to hold that sweet baby."

I swallowed the lump in my throat. "I'm a little under the weather," I lied. "I thought it might be better if I stayed away. You know, I don't want to get the baby sick, too."

"Oh, honey. I'm so sorry. Do we need to come home?"

I chuckled. "Of course not. I have a cold. I'm fine. Really, I've got a nice fire going and a new book to read. I'm looking forward to the day."

"Good. Your dad wants to talk to you. Bye."

"Bye, Mom."

There was some shuffling, and her dad's voice boomed through the cell phone. "Hey, kitten. Merry Christmas."

"Merry Christmas to you. Mom sounds so happy. Says you guys are having a wonderful time."

He chuckled. "We are. Should have done this years ago. That's one of the things I want to talk to you about when we get home. But I was wondering about the Montana trip. How did it go?"

"Great. Just great. I should have a proposal put together for your review by the time you get home. The people I met with were great." I winced. Everything was great, great, great. "They gave me everything I needed to put together a strong bid. I feel good about it."

I might be a little conflicted with lying to and sleeping with an ex-boyfriend, but otherwise, everything is great!

"Well, that sounds perfect. I knew you'd have no trouble handling the company reins. Well, I need to run. Your mother is dragging me out on another tour. Take care of yourself."

"You too, Dad. Merry Christmas."

I clicked off. Their call was exactly what I needed to pull my head out of the clouds and back down to earth. Now that Michael's parents had arrived, it was time for me to head home. One call to the airlines, and I had my ticket rebooked for that day. I packed the items I'd brought and those I'd purchased into my suitcase then had to sit on it to get it zipped. With a deep inhale and steely resolve, I opened the bedroom door. I was relieved to be met with an empty living room, the only sound being a low crackle from the fire. The mattress was gone. The room had been set back to rights.

Then I heard a clang from the kitchen. Following the noise, I found Michael's mother basting a turkey. She slid the bird back into the oven, wiped her hands on a dish towel, and looked at me.

"Michael's not here. He and his dad took the snowmobiles and rifles out to do some target shooting."

I nodded. "Okay."

She gestured toward my bag. "Going somewhere?"

I shrugged. "I need to get home. I've got a ton of work to get done before the end of the year. Now that y'all are here, Michael won't be alone." I pasted a smile on my face. "I am thankful he was here to save me from sleeping in the airport."

Her lips tightened. "Yes, you are quite fortunate."

"Well, I have my flight arranged for today, so…"

She frowned. "Today? Christmas?"

My fake smile made my cheeks quiver. "Perfect day to fly. Airports are less crowded, as are the planes, so it was a snap to get rebooked from my canceled flight." I checked the time on my phone. "Do you know if I can get a taxi out here?"

His mother untied her apron and laid it over the back of a chair. "You can't, no." She sighed loudly. "If you're determined to leave, I'll drive you, but are you sure you don't want to wait to talk with Michael before you go?"

I shook my head. "No. I think we said probably more than we should have a few minutes ago. I'd appreciate the ride, if it isn't too much trouble."

"I have to pick up his sister and her family anyway. What time is your flight?"

I told her, and she nodded. "Perfect timing. Let me get my purse, and I'll drive you there and pick up Patti at the same time." She opened a drawer and pulled out paper and a pen. "At least, leave him a note."

I did as she requested, not giving much more than a thank-you-for-your-help sort of message. I figured everyone in his family would see what I wrote, and I didn't want to make a big production out of leaving. A quiet exit really was more my style. If only Roy had understood that a couple of months ago.

Once we were in the car and on the way, his mother said, "Please don't take this the wrong way, but Michael was hurt the last time you two broke up, and I assume he will be this time. Maybe you leaving now, before things get too involved, is the best thing."

My stomach flipped over. I was mad and embarrassed. "Don't worry. I won't be contacting him."

"Understand, dear, I really think you're a delightful girl. Smart. Attractive. Professionally driven. But Michael needs a woman more from his world. You know. Simple needs. Someone who'd be happy as a wife and mother. Someone who'd enjoy family gatherings and backyard parties." She glanced over at me. "Please understand that I love my son. I only want what is best for him."

Tears burned in my eyes even as rage gnawed at my belly. "I get it, Mrs. Rockland. You've warned me away from your son. Like you said, I'm smart. You don't have to tell me twice."

"Oh, Mae. This isn't coming out the way I mean it. You are honestly a wonderful person. I just worry that, long-term, you'd find our lives to be so much more boring than you're used to. We aren't in the social circles you run in. Michael adores you, I'm sure of that, but your world just isn't our world." Her face was drawn and sad as she spoke. "I had hoped that once you married into the Livingston family, he'd be able to find a woman to settle down with. I think he compares every woman to you and always finds them lacking in some way." She glanced my way with a cheerless smile. "Apparently, you are a hard act to follow."

I shook my head. "You're wrong. Michael was the one who broke up with me. He's the one who's stayed away. I'm not hard to find. If he'd held on to old feelings for me, he could have easily contacted me. Don't worry. I'm sure he'll be fine."

However, it was me I was worried about. Would I be fine?

Chapter 13

Mae

He didn't call. I hadn't really expected him to. I'm sure his parents spent all of Christmas telling him how lucky he was that he'd only lost a couple of days with me before I'd walked out on him, which I did...but I didn't. Staying there had been impossible for me, especially after he'd actually verbalized how he felt about my parents.

"I thought I'd move this to the entry hall. Does that work for you?"

I jerked from my musings and looked at the party planner holding a tall vase of flowers. "Sure. You know I'm not that picky about stuff."

She smiled. "I know. That's why I love working with you." She set the vase on an entry hall table and returned to where I was sitting in my living room. "Can we go over the schedule for tonight?"

I closed my computer and nodded. "Shoot."

Molly, the party planner my family had used forever, pulled a folder from her ever-present tote bag. "The caterer will be here in an hour. The bartenders will be here at six. The musical quartet will be here at six-thirty for set up and begin playing at seven, or earlier if needed. They will take a break at eight and ten and play until twelve-thirty. By that time, I'm thinking most of your guests will be headed out. If not, maybe no music will signal that it's time to go." She laughed.

I answered her laugh with a polite chuckle. I wish I hadn't let KatiLyn talk me into this New Year's Eve bash. I would rather have been in my pajamas watching the ball drop on television.

We reviewed the food, not that I cared what was served. Everything had tasted like cardboard for the past week.

"And I'll be back about seven," Molly said.

"Remember to have a good time while you're here," I told her. "Is your husband coming with you?"

She nodded. "He said he'd help keep an eye out for guests who imbibe a little too heavily."

I nodded. "Good."

Molly stood. "I guess, that's it. I'm headed home to get dressed."

I walked her to the door. "Thank you. You've done a great job putting this party together."

"Hey, I love working with your family. You're all so easy to please."

After she was gone, I flopped back on the sofa. I

still had some time before the caterer arrived. I opened my computer and began reading the Bozeman airport proposal. My phone lit up with a call from KatiLyn.

"Ready for tonight?" she asked. "Can I do anything?"

"Molly the Magnificent has everything under control. You bringing Ted? Or is it Jack, this week?"

She laughed. "New guy. You haven't met him. Craig Boston."

"Nope. That's a new one."

"Who's your date tonight?"

I winced. "I never got around to asking anyone. Besides, I'm the hostess. I'll be flitting around all evening. I don't need a date."

KatiLyn clicked her tongue. "Can I ask a favor then?"

"Let me guess. Craig has a friend, and you want to fix me up. Nope. Not tonight."

She gave an exasperated sigh. "No. It's Charlie."

"Your brother?"

"Yeah. His girlfriend broke up with him."

"She hook up with another guy? That sucks."

"Well, actually, another girl. She's decided she's gay."

My eyebrows shot up. "Seriously?"

"Yeah. He's really bummed out. I thought maybe he could come along and be your date."

"Sure. I love Charlie, and besides, it'll help my reputation to be seen with a younger guy."

KatiLyn chuckled. "Thanks. Don't be surprised if he's all droopy and sad."

"Not for long. I'll drag him around with me all

evening. I'll make sure he has a good time. There will probably be a single gal or two I can introduce him to."

"Great. Gotta run. See you about seven."

At five, I let the caterers in and headed to my room to dress. I'd bought a sparkly red dress for this evening, and while I wasn't feeling so sparkly, I decided that it would be best to fake it 'til I felt it.

When my bartenders arrived at six to set up, my makeup and hair team came in behind them. I realized having my hair and makeup done by professionals tonight was overkill, but there was no way I could hide the dark circles under my eyes. They could.

By six-forty-five, I'd been brushed, fluffed, and buffed within an inch of my life. Looking in the mirror, I decided I looked better than I had for my non-wedding. I might be a tad sad, but I wasn't nervous. The flirty, red dress boosted my self-confidence one-thousand percent.

As my makeup team left, KatiLyn entered, followed by her brother and her date, the mysterious Craig Boston. He was tall, red-headed with a red beard and blue eyes. A total cutie.

"I'm Mae," I said, extending my hand.

"Craig. Nice to meet you."

"You, too. So glad you could make it tonight."

He glanced around. "Great place."

"Thank you." I hugged KatiLyn, and then Charlie. "You two spiff up quite nicely," I said jokingly.

KatiLyn wore turquoise-blue pants and a low-cut, very daring multi-colored blouse. She turned in a circle, and I saw the back was lower cut than the front.

"I hope you've got those tatas taped down, so they don't come flopping out while you're dancing."

She threw her head back in a laugh. "Of course. I might look slutty, but I don't act slutty." She looked at her date. "Hands off the merchandise tonight, bud."

He laughed and put his arm around her. "Yes, ma'am. Now, which way to the bar?"

They headed off, and I looked at Charlie. At twenty-two, he hadn't fully reached the handsome man he would become. However, his gawky teen look was way in the past.

I whistled. "Damn. You're looking good."

He smiled, but it didn't come close to reaching his eyes. "Thanks for taking pity on me, Mae."

I tsked. "Don't be ridiculous. I don't have pity for you in the least. I needed a date. I should be groveling my thanks for stepping in, so I didn't have to be dateless at my own party."

"Thank you for saying that," he said.

"Now, you hang on to me all night." I slipped my arm through his. "Every woman under the age of fifty will be so jealous of me."

"What's wrong with the ones over fifty?" he asked with a grin.

I arched a brow. "They weren't invited."

The doorbell rang, and the hired staff opened the door and began admitting my guests. By ten, the caterer had circled my condo with numerous trays of food. I made sure all the guests were eating as much as they were drinking. The liquor flowed freely, even if my bartenders were weakening the drinks now. Not that I couldn't afford the booze, but I wanted to ensure no one got totally out of hand tonight.

I'd lost Charlie to a couple of single women closer to his age than mine. I checked on him a few times, but he wasn't missing me at all. That made me happy.

At eleven, the biggest surprise of the evening walked in. My parents arrived home a couple of days early. Dad said they'd missed me so much, and Mom was ready to see her own bed again.

I hugged both of them tightly. "Man, am I glad to see you," I said.

"You too, honey," Mom said. "You don't mind that we crashed your party?"

I laughed. "I'll send you a bill for the two bites of food you'll eat and the one glass of wine you'll drink."

She giggled. "We might have already had a few glasses of champagne on the plane over."

I rolled my eyes. My parents regressed to teenagers with a couple of bottles of champagne.

"Well, let me get you another glass," I said and walked them to the bar.

"How's the business going? You enjoy being the one in charge?" Dad asked as we waited for the champagne.

"Now, Gordon, you promised you wouldn't talk business tonight," my mom chided.

"It was just a question, Alice."

"Everything's fine, Dad. I'll be glad to have you back in the office next week."

My parents exchanged glances, and I wondered if Dad had been trying the job out on me for size. "You are coming back, right?" I asked Dad.

He patted my shoulder. "We'll talk next week." He laughed. "Don't look so horrified. I'm not walking out on you."

"Whew," I said.

"Let's dance, Gordon." My mother drained her champagne glass like it was a chugging contest and pulled my dad toward the music.

I could only hope to have a marriage like theirs. I could see now that Roy and I would never have had a relationship like that. I put my party smile back on and began mingling around the room.

Charlie grabbed my hand as I passed. "Dance? It's almost midnight, and I thought I'd like to spend it with you."

"Of course." I looked at the two women. "Excuse me, ladies. You don't mind if I take my date back now, do you?"

He took my right hand and put his other hand low on my waist. We moved into the dancers.

"I'm sorry," I said, giving him a smile. "I didn't realize you needed rescuing. I'd have been back sooner. I thought you were enjoying yourself."

He shrugged. "I am enjoying myself. But I wanted a minute of your time to thank you."

"I'm so glad you came."

"Me too," he said and dipped me.

I laughed as I looked up from my bent position. It was then that my front door opened, and my second surprise of the evening entered.

Dressed in jeans, thick-soled motorcycle boots, and a flannel shirt, Michael Rockland strode in like he'd been invited. His eyes flashed around the room, landing on me and Charlie. His strong jaw tightened as our gazes met.

Charlie righted me so the blood was no longer rushing to my brain. My heart, however, wasn't sure how to react. It definitely picked up its pace. My breath caught in my throat. My vision tunneled down to him. The rest of the room and all its people vanished.

"Michael," I whispered.

Chapter 14

Rock

W *ell, hell.*
She sure hadn't wasted any time replacing me. Seeing as she'd walked out on me only seven days ago, she'd obviously had this date planned. Nobody rounded up a New Year's Eve date in only a week.

She stared at me from across the room, still in the arms of her date...or was he her new lover? Jealousy and anger flooded me. If the look on her face was any indication, she hadn't expected me to follow her home. I shouldn't have. I'd made a horrible mistake.

I turned to leave when a hand touched my arm. I looked down, as familiar with those fingers as I was my own. How had she made it across the room so quickly?

"Michael."

I looked at her. Damn. She was fucking gorgeous. Her blonde hair shone under the room's lighting. Her mid-thigh dress glittered with each breath she took.

"This was a mistake," I growled. "I'll leave."

"No," she said, tightening her fingers on my arm. "Don't go."

I looked around and saw people were watching us as though we were the entertainment for the evening. KatiLyn started marching toward us, as did Mae's parents. Maybe they'd join forces to toss me out. It'd take all of them. Mae had asked me to not go, and I wasn't going...not until she ordered me out.

"What are you doing here?" KatiLyn said the second she was within ear shot.

"I've got this," Mae said.

"Honey," her father said with a frown. "Why is your mechanic here?"

"Dad. That was uncalled for." She glared at him.

Her father shrugged with confusion, as though he had no idea what he'd said that was so offensive.

Her mother stepped forward. "I remember you. Michael, isn't it?" She held out her hand to me. "It's been a long time. How are you doing?"

I shook her hand even as I wanted to howl in anger and frustration. Could it be more obvious that I didn't belong here? The rich people. The fancy people. While I probably had more money than some in this room, I felt judged and found lacking.

Her date rested his hand on her shoulder. "Mae, can I help?"

Her jaw tightened. I could see the muscle tic in her cheek. "I've got this," she said. "KatiLyn, can you play hostess until I return?"

Mae took my hand and led me out of the room to her home office. The door closed with a solid click. I glanced around at the simple furnishings. A desk. A file cabinet. A recliner. Framed diplomas dotted the wall above the desk. A sliding door that led to a balcony.

I gestured toward the balcony door. "Gonna toss me out?"

She snorted. "I should. I really should. What are you doing here?"

"You left me. In Montana. You didn't say a word. Just left."

"What was there to say? We knew our time together wasn't reality. We knew it was limited."

She shrugged, and it looked so much like her father's action. She was her father's daughter.

"I appreciate all you did for me. I-I enjoyed our time."

I snorted in disgust. "You enjoyed our time? How polite."

With tight lips and a glare, she stomped her foot. "What do you want me to say?"

"Fuck." I raked my fingers through my hair.

She walked to the sliding door and stared out at the city lights. "We have no future...at least not together." With a sad laugh and chuckle, she continued, "Remember how you said my parents didn't like you? Well, your mother let me know in no uncertain terms that, while I was good enough for you to fool around with, I am not her choice for you to settle down with."

She turned to look at me. "We are the Capulets and Montagues."

I took a step toward her. "Except we aren't teenagers still controlled by our parents. We're adults who direct our own lives."

"You were at my wedding, right?"

I nodded, not sure where she was going with this.

"Did you hear what my father said? He and Mom will love and accept the man I love. They weren't crazy about Roy, but if that's who I wanted to spend my life with, they would've made him part of the family."

"I heard what he said."

"But your mother..." She sighed. "She made it clear that I didn't fit into your world."

I frowned. "Exactly what did she say?"

She shrugged again. "That I'm too snooty to be happy with a simple family life." She smiled. "I might be paraphrasing a little, but that was the gist of it."

"I'm pretty sure that's not what she meant."

"Doesn't matter, Michael."

I took another step toward her. "It does matter. Do you know why I left ten years ago?" I held up my hand to keep her from answering. "Even if you think you do, here's the truth. You were out of my class, socially and financially. I saw those guys at college. I couldn't compete with their smarts and their futures."

She waved a hand. "Ridiculous."

"Maybe, but walking away from you was the hardest thing I've ever done. Mom saw how much it killed me to leave you. I'm sure she was just being protective."

She shrugged. "I hear what you're saying, but she

made me think, take stock of what I do want in life. She was right about a lot of things. I love my job. I'm proud of the company my dad built. I want to run it and take it to the next level. I love living in Dallas. I love living in this building in downtown. I'm not looking for the house with the white picket fence and two-point-five kids. Hell, Michael, I'm not sure I want children. I know for sure I don't want them now."

His eyebrows lowered. "Who said I wanted children, a house, a yard and a white picket fence?"

"Your mother."

"Instead of leaving, did you think about asking me what I wanted?"

She raised both eyebrows and gave me a hard stare. "Instead of leaving me ten years ago, did you think about asking me what I wanted?"

My breath caught. I shook my head. "Touché."

She took a step toward me. My heart raced.

"We've been letting others tell us what we should be doing, what we should want," she said, her gaze locking with mine.

I nodded. "We've let others' opinions influence our actions."

"Whether those opinions were correct or not."

I lifted an eyebrow. "Even if those opinions were real or simply impressions we formed in our minds and held on to, we are in control of our own lives."

Our gazes held.

"So, what now?" she asked.

"Now, I go home, you finish your party, and I'll call you."

She shook her head. "Wrong answer." She wound her arms around my neck.

I wrapped mine around her waist. "Oh yeah?"

At that moment, fireworks began shooting all over the city. A celebratory cry rose from the living room.

"It's a new year," she said.

"It's a new beginning," I said, and then kissed her. Her lips tasted like strawberries and cream.

Someone groaned. It might have been me.

Our tongues met. Mine glided along the side of hers into her warm mouth. We kissed long and hard, neither of us apparently ready to give up...not the kiss nor on us.

"I love you," I said, against her lips. "I've always loved you."

Her eyes glittered as she looked up at me. "I thought I'd moved on with my life. I'd been ready to settle with Roy, and trust me, it was settling. But I thought you hadn't wanted me."

"I wanted you," I said, while a desire so fierce it burned my throat, rose inside me. "I wanted you more than I wanted air, but I wanted what was best for you. I was stupid enough to believe it couldn't be me. I didn't think I could be enough."

She kissed me firmly. "You were so stupid."

"Still am. I let you leave Montana without me."

"You didn't have a choice there. I took that choice away from you."

I sighed and rested my forehead on hers. "We've lost a lot of time. I want to ask you to marry me, but that sounds crazy."

Nodding, she said, "It does. I think I'm still in love with you, Michael, but it's been just over two months since I was ready to marry someone else."

I gripped her upper arms and gave her a little

shake. "So, date me. Take me home to your parents' house. I'll take you to mine. Let's find out if what we feel is real, not that I really have to. I know I love you. I've never met any woman who compared to you."

She chuckled. "Your mother told me you compared all women to me and none of them measured up."

"That's because none of them were you. I've never felt what I feel for you for anyone else. You're special." I hesitated, but she had to know. "You are my heart and soul, Mae. Without you, I am hollow."

A tear rolled down her cheek. "Oh, Michael, I've never loved anyone the way I loved you."

"So, we'll see where this goes?" I asked, my voice deep with nerves. If she said no, then I wasn't sure what I'd do.

Chapter 15

Mae

We exited my office hand-in-hand, surprised to not encounter any of my friends or family in the hall. I had wondered if KatiLyn had her ear pressed to the door. Either she had and could make an exceptionally quiet escape, or she hadn't been there at all. It would be months before I got the answer to that question. She'd been trying to listen until her date—bless him—pulled her away.

My parents, KatiLyn, her date Craig, and Charlie, my date, sat in my living room, drinks in hand, casually discussing the upcoming college football bowls. Call me suspicious, but all five of them looked like they were sitting on sticks of dynamite.

"Where's everyone?" I asked.

"Gone. The bar closed at twelve-twenty, per your request. The caterers left shortly thereafter. The rest of the party followed the booze out the door. So, it's just us." KatiLyn announced all this as though nothing were amiss.

I'd never seen five people trying so hard not to ask questions.

"Well, thanks for coming," I said, still holding Michael's hand.

Charlie stood first. "Thank you for being my date tonight." When he kissed my cheek, I felt Michael's fingers tighten, and I grinned.

"Good luck, Charlie. You never know how things will work out with your ex."

"Not sure I want to." He smiled. "I've got a late date, so I'd better hustle."

I laughed as he hurried to the door. He exited with a backwards wave.

"I guess we need to get going," KatiLyn's date said and stood. Her date was more focused on getting her out of there, and then out of her clothes than whether I held the hand of a man who'd crashed the party.

She remained seated until he pulled her to standing.

"Say good night and thank you to the nice hostess," he said to KatiLyn.

She tossed him a glare and a snarl. He just laughed.

I liked this guy. The first one who didn't let KatiLyn have her way all the time.

"If you need me, need anything, just call," she whispered into my ear as she hugged me. "I'll call you tomorrow."

"Not too early," I said.

She looked at Michael and back to me. "We'll see. Good night, Rock."

"Back atcha, KatiLyn," he replied.

Then it was just my parents, Michael, and me. We sat on the couch across from them, a glass coffee table separating us.

Mom was smiling. Being a good Southern-bred woman, she was using her bright facial expression to hide her confusion as to why I was holding hands with someone who hadn't been my date. Later, she explained she'd also been confused that I hadn't been all that concerned when my date had announced his late date and left.

"Why do I feel like I've just walked into the last five minutes of a five-hour mini-series?" Mom asked. "What am I missing?"

"Well, Mom, it's like this. Michael and I used to date in high school."

"I know that, dear. I remember him well. You've really grown into a handsome man," she said to Michael. "Not that I'm surprised." She winked at him, and I almost fell off the cushions. "You were such a cute boy." She looked back at me, then at Dad and back at me. "So, is someone going to fill me in on what's happening?" She looked at Dad. "Honey?"

"I'll start," I said. "The one and only time I brought Michael home to our house, Dad took the time to warn Michael off dating me. Dad felt that he wasn't good enough for his little princess."

"That's not exactly what I said," Dad protested.

"That's the message you sent," I said, giving him a pointed look.

His face wore a mask of bewilderment. "I think you misunderstood," he said to Michael. "What did I say?"

Michael cleared his throat. "It seems so stupid now. You talked about Mae, how proud you were of her, how she was going places in life. You talked about how you hoped she would join your company and take over some day. You asked me about what I was going to do, where I was going to college." He sighed and squeezed my hands. "As I repeat our discussion, I can see it from a completely different slant. As an eighteen-year-old in the throes of his first, well..." He glanced at me and then back at Dad, "my first brush with love, my insecurities were through the roof. I was sure you could see me for the middle-class guy I was and probably would always be. I didn't feel worthy of Mae, and what I heard, what I latched onto, was that I wasn't in your social class and never would be. In short, I wasn't good enough for her."

My dad dropped heavily against the back of the sofa. "Wow. That's a lot to take in."

"Did you tell him he wasn't good enough for me?" I asked.

Mom took Dad's hand in a gesture of support.

"I don't think I said those exact words. It was probably more of an attitude than what I actually said." My dad shook his head and then sighed. "It wasn't that I didn't think Michael was good enough for you. I didn't think any *boy* was right for you. I didn't want you to tie yourself down at that age. I wanted you to go to college, see the world, and have some fun before you settled down." He looked at Michael. "I could see how she felt about you whenever you were around. I heard her talk about you to her girlfriends. I knew she was falling in love with you, but I also realized you were both so young and had so much time ahead of you. I *am* sorry you were hurt by my words and actions. I was doing what I thought was best for my daughter and although she's an adult, I still try to do what I hope is the right thing for her."

"And yet, you were going to let me marry Roy?" I laughed so they would know I was kidding.

Mom shook her head. "I had to hold your dad back a few times when Roy visited."

I blinked at that. "So, neither of you liked Roy?"

"He's okay," Dad said, wrinkling his nose. "But I never felt like he was the right one for you."

"I confess," Mom said, "I wanted to intervene, but you are an adult, and as such, entitled to make your own mistakes. But honestly, you didn't smile much. You never had a sparkle in your eye around him—not like you do now."

Michael squeezed my fingers.

"So, is that why you're here, Michael?" Mom asked. "To get back with our Mae?"

Chapter 16

Mae

Christmas Eve - Thirty-Five Years Later

"And then what happened, Grandma?"

I smiled down at the five adorable children sitting on the floor around my feet. Each one was dressed in special matching Christmas Eve pajamas I'd had made for them. Every year either Michael or I have to tell them the story of how we met and fell in love. This year, Michael and I shared the storytelling duties.

Beside me on the sofa, Michael draped his arm around me as I replied, "Well, I made your Grandpa court me."

"And did she ever," Michael, my husband, my love, my soul answered.

Four-year-old Aiden, our son's son, wrinkled his brow. "What does court mean?"

Before either of us could answer, Polly Ann, our oldest granddaughter at nine, said, "That means she made him take her on dates and buy her dinner and try to kiss her."

"Polly Ann," Laura, my daughter exclaimed. "Who told you about kissing?"

The towheaded child looked up at her mother— my oldest daughter—with pure innocence. "Grandpa."

"Dad!" Laura said, giving her dad a stern look. "I asked you to censure those stories."

Michael just chuckled. "Without those kisses, you wouldn't be here, Laura." When our son, Tony laughed, Michael added, "or you either."

"That's enough," I said. I looked down at our grandchildren. "So, that's how your grandpa and I got together."

"But that's not all," Polly Ann insisted. "Tell them about your wedding."

Michael and I exchanged glances before I continued. "Your grandfather did such a good job taking me out on dates, that I knew we had to get married. So, we got married on Valentine's Day. Do you know when that is?"

"In February," Polly Ann shouted. "I get to give out valentines to everyone in my class."

I nodded. "That's right. You do."

"Okay, that's enough stories for tonight," Laura said. "You guys need to get to bed so Santa can come."

Then there were five screaming children, hopping and running around our living room, excited that Santa would be bringing them presents tonight. As they settled into their beds—which was no easy feat —Michael and I went from room to room hugging them and kissing them good night.

When we got to Polly Ann's bed, she asked, "Where did you and Grandpa get married? Were there a bunch of people there?"

I sat on the edge of her bed to answer her question. Polly Ann was like our daughter. She was smart and inquisitive. A devoted reader, she would read anything, but lately, Nancy Drew was holding her attention. She was entering that cycle of life where boys weren't so icky anymore and was asking more questions about me and Michael and about her own mom and dad. But that's another story.

"Grandpa and I got married in a small chapel made from wood and glass. This chapel stands deep into the woods, so when people marry, all the forest animals come and watch."

"Who was there?"

"All of our family and friends."

"No, I mean, what animals came?"

"Oh, well, let's see. There were deer. A few rabbits came by. A big owl hooted through our ceremony, too."

Her eyes widened. "Were there any bears?"

I snuggled the covers around her. "No bears."

She yawned. "I'm glad you married Grandpa."

I looked up at Michael, who stood with his hand on my shoulder. "Me, too, Polly."

Later that evening, after our adult children had

put out the Santa gifts for their children and departed for their beds, Michael and I sat on the sofa and watched the lights twinkle on our live blue spruce tree. No decorator would have claimed the tangle of lights or the imperfect placement of ornaments, not to mention the clumps of icicles thrown on the branches by our grandchildren. Our tree would never make the Dallas society pages, but to me, it was beautiful, just like our lives had been.

I sighed, and my love wrapped his arms around me. "Just how I love to spend Christmas," I said, leaning my face against his. "In your arms."

ABOUT THE AUTHOR

 New York Times and USA Today Bestselling Author Cynthia D'Alba was born and raised in a small Arkansas town. After being gone for a number of years, she's thrilled to be making her home back in Arkansas living on the banks of an eight-thousand acre lake.

Photo by Annie Ray

When she's not reading or writing or plotting, she's doorman for her spoiled border collie, cook, housekeeper and chief bottle washer for her husband and slave to a noisy, messy parrot. She loves to chat online with friends and fans.

Send snail mail to: Cynthia D'Alba PO Box 2116 Hot Springs, AR 71914

Or better yet! She would for you to take her news-letter. She promises not to spam you, not to fill your inbox with advertising, and not to sell your name and email address to anyone. Check her website for a link to her newsletter.

www.cynthiadalba.com
https://cynthiadalba.com/newsletter-sign-up/
cynthiadalba@gmail.com

facebook.com/cynthiadalba

twitter.com/cynthiadalba

bookbub.com/profile/cynthia-d-alba

goodreads.com/CynthiaDAlba

amazon.com/Cynthia-DAlba

instagram.com/cynthiadalba

Thank for you reading Christmas in His Arms.

The best thing you can do for any author is to leave a review wherever you bought this book.

And keep up with me through my newsletter!

Thanks!
Cynthia

~

~

Keep reading for excerpts from other Dallas Debutante books.

Hot SEAL, Black Coffee
A Dallas Debutante/SEALs in Paradise/McCool
Trilogy (Book 1)

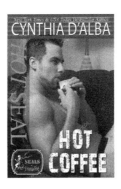

Dealing with a sexy ex-girlfriend, a jewel heist, and a murder-for-hire can make an ex-SEAL bodyguard a tad cranky.

Trevor Mason accepts what should be a simple job...protect the jewels his ex-girlfriend will wear to a breast cancer fundraiser. As founder and owner of Eye Spy International, he should send one of his guys, but he needs to get his ex out of his system and this is the perfect opportunity to remind himself that she is a spoiled, rich debutante who dumped him with a Dear John letter during his SEAL training.

Respected breast cancer doctor Dr. Risa McCool hates being in the limelight for her personal life. Her life's work is breast cancer treatment and research, which she'd rather be known for than for her carefree, partying debutante years. She agrees to be the chairperson for the annual breast cancer fundraiser even though it means doing publicity appearances and interviews, all while wearing the famous pink Breast Cancer Diamond for each public event. The multi-million dollar value of the pink stone requires an armed bodyguard at all times.

Past attractions flame, proving to be a distraction to the serious reality of the situation. When Risa and the millions in diamonds go missing, nothing will stop Trevor from bringing her home, with or without the jewels.

∿

At two-thirty Monday afternoon, Dr. Risa McCool's world shifted on its axis. He was back. She wasn't ready. But then, would she ever be ready?

Four hours passed before she was able to disengage from work and go home. As she pulled under the portico of her high-rise building and the condo valet hurried out to park her eight-year-old sedan, her stomach roiled at the realization that Trevor Mason—high school and college boyfriend and almost fiancé—would be waiting for her in her condo, or at least should be. She pressed a shaking hand to her abdomen and inhaled a deep, calming breath. It didn't work. There was still a slight quiver to her hands as she grabbed her purse and briefcase from the passenger seat.

She paused to look in the mirror. A tired brunette looked back at her. Dark circles under her eyes. Limp hair pulled into a ponytail at the back of her head. Pale lips. Paler cheeks. Not one of her better looks.

Would he be the same? Tall with sun-kissed hair and mesmerizing azure-blue eyes?

Tall, sure. That was a given.

Eye color would have to be the same, but his sun-bleached hair? His muscular physique? In high school and college, he'd played on the offense for their high school and college football teams, but she had never really understood what he did. Sometimes he ran and sometimes he hit other guys. What she remembered were strong arms and a wide chest. Would those be the same?

Almost fifteen years had passed since she'd last seen him. He hadn't come back for their tenth nor their fifteenth high school reunions. The explanation for his absences involved SEAL missions to who knew where. Risa had wondered if she'd ever see him again, whether he'd make it through all his deployments and secret ops.

Well, he had and now she had to work with him.

She took a deep breath and slid from the car.

"Good Evening, Dr. McCool," the valet said.

"Evening, John. Do you know if my guest arrived?"

"Yes, ma'am. About four hours ago."

"Do you know if the groceries were delivered?"

"Yes, ma'am. Cleaning service has also been in."

"Thank you. Have a nice evening."

"You, too."

She acknowledged the guard on duty at the desk with a nod and continued to the private residents-only elevator that opened to a back-door entrance to her condo. After putting her key in the slot, she pressed the button for the forty-first floor and then leaned against the wall for the ride.

Her anxiety at seeing Trevor climbed as the elevator dinged past each floor. It was possible, even probable, that she had made a mistake following her mother's advice to employ his company. She was required to have a bodyguard for every public event since the announcement of the pink Breast Cancer Diamond. Her insurance company insisted on it. The jewelry designer demanded it. And worse, her mother was adamant on a guard. How did one say no to her mother?

Plus, as head of the Dallas Area Breast Cancer Research Center, she'd been tasked with wearing that gaudy necklace with a pink diamond big enough to choke a horse for the annual fundraising gala. The damn thing was worth close to fifteen or twenty million and was heavy as hell. Who'd want it?

The elevator dinged one last time and the doors slid open. She stepped into a small vestibule and let herself into her place expecting to see Trevor.

Only, she didn't.

Instead there was music—jazz to be specific. She followed the sounds of Stan Getz to her balcony, her heart in her throat.

A man sat in a recliner facing the night lights of Dallas, a highball in one hand, a cigar in the other.

"I'm glad to see you stock the good bourbon," he said, lifting the glass, but not turning to face her. "And my brand, too. Should I be impressed?"

Her jaw clenched. Their fights had always been about money—what she had and what he didn't.

"I don't know," she said. "Are you impressed?"

He took a drag off the cigar and chased the smoke down his throat with a gulp of hundred-dollar bourbon. "Naw. You can afford it."

"Are you going to look at me or will my first conversation with you in fifteen years be with the back of your head?"

After stabbing out the cigar, he finished his drink, sat it on the tile floor, and rose. Lord, he was still as towering and overwhelming as she remembered him. At five-feet-ten-inches, Risa was tall, but Trevor's height made her feel positively petite. As he turned, every muscle in her body tensed as she stood unsure whether she was preparing to fight him, flee from him or fuck him.

"Hello, Risa."

Hot SEAL, Black Coffee
A Dallas Debutante/SEALs in Paradise/McCool
Trilogy (Book 3)

A sexy new book in the Dallas Debutantes/McCool
Family trilogy. All books in the trilogy can be read as
standalones.

*A cowboy who isn't what he appears must play
private host to a spoiled Dallas Debutante who isn't what
she seems. Between frozen pipes, bonfires, bowling, a flu
epidemic, a jealous ex-girlfriend and a snowstorm of the
century, when will they ever find time to discover the real
person under their façade?*

After an embarrassing disaster at her cousin's
wedding, Dr. Wendy McCool needs a change of scene
and some quiet time to reflect on her medical career
choices, her future and her lack of a love life...or
really, any life outside of eighty-hour work weeks. An

offer of a private apartment from her mother's friend sends her off to Montana only to discover the unexpected.

Over a decade in Chicago as a hedge fund manager and Zane Miller is ready to call it quits. He misses the family ranch in Montana, the fresh mountain air, and even the smell of a barn full of horses. When his mother falls ill, he heads to Montana, ready to do what it takes to get her health back, even running the ranch while his parents winter in Florida. What he didn't agree to was playing host to a spoiled Dallas Debutante/jilted bride. Heaven help him.

Hot SEAL, Alaskan Nights
A Dallas Debutante/SEALs in Paradise Novel

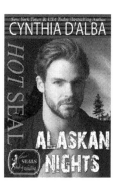

From NYT and USA Today Best Selling Author comes a beach read that isn't the typical sun-drenched location. Homer, Alaska. A Navy SEAL on leave. A nurse practitioner in seclusion. A jealous ex-lover looking for redemption...or is it revenge?

Navy SEAL Levi Van der Hayden, aka Dutch, returns to his family home in Homer, AK for the three Rs...rest, relaxation and recovery. As the only SEAL injured during his team's last mission, the last thing he wants to do is show his bullet wound to friends... it's in his left gluteus maximus and he's tired of being the butt of all the jokes (his own included.)

After a violent confrontation with a controlling, narcissistic ex-lover, nurse practitioner Bailey Brown flees Texas for Alaska. A maternal grandmother still in residence provides her with the ideal sanctuary... still in the U.S. but far enough away to escape her ex's reach.

Attracted to the cute nurse from his welcome

home beach party, Levi insists on showing her the real Alaska experience. When her safety is threatened, he must use all his SEAL skills to protect her and eliminate the risk, even if it means putting his own life on the line.

~

Levi Van der Hayden's left butt cheek was on fire. He shifted uncomfortably in the back seat of the subcompact car masquerading as their Uber ride. As soon as he moved, the stitches in his left thigh reminded him that pushing off with that leg was also mistake.

"We should try to get upgraded when we get to the airport," Compass said.

Compass, also known as Levi's best friend Rio North, was going way out of his way to help Levi get home leave, but at this moment, Levi gritted his teeth at the ridiculous suggestion.

"I don't have the money for that and you know it." Levi, aka Dutch to his SEAL team buds, knew he shouldn't be so grumpy what with all Compass was doing for him but damn it! Why did he have to be shot in the ass? The guys would never let him live it down.

He repositioned his hips so most of the weight was on his uninjured right butt cheek.

"You bring anything for the pain, Dutch?"

"Took something about an hour ago, which right now seems like last week."

The car stopped at the Departure gates of San Diego International Airport. Dutch climbed from the back seat of the way-too-tiny car with a few choice cuss words and stood on the sidewalk. Compass paid the driver and then hefted out two duffle bags. After slinging both onto his shoulders, he gestured toward the airport with his chin.

Once inside, Compass said, "Seriously Dutch, you need to upgrade. There is no way you are going to be able to stretch out and you know what the doctor said about pulling those stitches."

Levi glared at his friend and answered him with a one-finger response.

Compass grinned back him. "All joking aside, I'll pay for your upgrade. Your ass literally *needs* to be in first class." The asshole then leaned back and glanced down at Levi's ass...well actually the cheek where he'd been shot coming back from their last fucking mission.

"No, damn it, Compass, I already told you I can't afford it and I'm not accepting charity." Levi knew his friend could afford to upgrade Levi to a big, roomy, first-class seat, but he was already taking Compass way out of his way with this trip. When his friend opened his mouth to speak, Levi held up a hand to stop him. "Not even from you. I appreciate it, man, I really do, but no." Levi shook his head emphatically. "I fucking hate being such a pain in your ass, har har har."

To say Levi had been the target of his SEAL team buddies' relentless butt jokes would be an understatement. They'd been brutal in the way only people who love you can. Levi knew that. Understood that. And would have been there throwing out the butt and ass jokes if it'd been anyone else who'd gotten shot in the ass, but it wasn't. It was him and he was tired of it. He lowered himself carefully onto a bench.

Compass looked around and then back to Levi. "Okay, look, I'm going to go talk to the agent over there. I'm not spending a dime, but sometimes they let active duty get upgrades. Let me see what I can do. Okay?"

Levi followed Compass's gaze to an attractive brunette behind the Delta service counter. He chuckled. "Damn man, you could pick up a woman anywhere, couldn't you?"

Compass shrugged, but his grin said he knew exactly what Levi was talking about. "It's a God-given talent. But that's not what this is about. Give me your military ID."

Levi pulled out his card, but hesitated. Compass had more money than God, Dropping an thousand or so dollars to change a plane ticket was probably pocket change to him, but not to Levi.

Compass jerked Levi's military card out his hand with a snort. "Shit that damaged ass muscle has fucked up your reflexes."

"Fuck you, man. It's the pain meds." Levi narrowed his eyes at his best friend. "Not a penny, Compass, not a fucking penny. Got it?"

"Loud and clear." Compass pointed to him. "Stay here and look pathetic."

Compass had only taken a few steps before Levi heard him laugh. God damn asshole.

Jesus, he hated this. Not only was he in pain, but the damn doctors had restricted him from lifting anything over twenty pounds. Twenty pounds! Like he was some fucking girl or something. He was a Navy SEAL. He could lift twenty pounds with his toes...or could before just moving his toes made the exit wound on his thigh ache.

Now that their last mission was behind them—he groaned at his own bad joke—the team had a little time off, which meant he could finally go home for a few days. However, the restrictions from the doctors meant someone had to help him with his duffle bag since it definitely weighed more than twenty pounds. He was pissed off and embarrassed by that limit to his activities. Hell, even jogging was off his activities list until the stitches healed a little more.

He'd been ordered to do medical follow-up at the Alaskan VA Health Clinic. Knowing his commander, Skipper would follow up on that, and if Levi didn't follow orders, his ass would be grass. He groan again and ordered himself to stop with the ass jokes.

Turning his attention back to the action across the lobby Levi watched Compass operate. He was too far away to hear the conversation, but he knew his friend's M.O. well. He'd smile. He'd compliment the woman. Then he'd toss in his best friend's war wound for sympathy. Levi snorted to himself. He'd seen Compass in action too many times to count.

Compass leaned toward the Delta agent and Levi was sure the poor woman had been sucked into Compass's charismatic gravitational pull. She didn't stand a chance against a pro like Compass.

When Compass set both of their duffle bags on

the scale and the airline agent tagged them, Levi was at least sure he was going home. What he didn't know was if it would be in the front of the plane or the back of the plane. If it weren't for his ass and leg, he wouldn't care where he sat, but he knew that wasn't true for his friend, who always went first-class when he could.

Compass turned from the check-in desk and started toward Levi with a broad smile he'd seen before when Compass got what he wanted.

Levi eyed him. "Why do you have a shit-eating grin on your face? What did you do?"

"I'm smiling because I'm a fucking magic man." He handed Levi a boarding pass.

Levi studied the boarding pass with first class all in capital letters. "Did you buy this?" His lips tightened into a straight line.

Compass help up his hands. "Nope. Not a penny spent. I swear on my mother's grave."

"Your mother is alive, asshole."

"Yeah, but we have a family plot and we all have real estate allotted. I swear *I* didn't spend a single dime on that ticket man. That pretty little thing over there hooked you up." He motioned over to Brittany who was busy with another customer.

"Sir, are you ready?"

Levi's gaze fell on an attendant pushing a wheelchair. "What the fuck?"

Made in the USA
Columbia, SC
23 October 2021

47406140R10104